PRAISE FOR

It Is Wood, It Is Stone

"Debut novelist Gabriella Burnham knocks it out of the park with a sharp, knotty novel about colorism and class in the heart of São Paulo. Left adrift after moving from America to Brazil for her husband Dennis's work, Linda develops a fraught relationship with the couple's maid, Marta, whose roots at Linda and Dennis's home run deeper than either American can imagine."

—*Harper's Bazaar,* Best Books of 2020

"[A] captivating novel about an American woman, Linda, who moves to São Paulo with her husband . . . Linda's behavior grows erratic after she becomes attracted to a woman, and she describes her self-dissociation in painstaking, Lispector-esque clarity. Burnham's ever-tense domestic drama becomes an awe-inspiring study of gaps between race and class."

—*Publishers Weekly,* Best Fiction Books of 2020

"The substance of Burnham's artful tapestry of a novel . . . concerns Linda's relationships with other women. Marta, a black woman appointed by the university as the couple's maid, brings Linda into direct confrontation with her own privilege as an affluent white woman abroad. Soon Linda becomes infatuated with Celia, a mysterious artist she meets in a bar, and finds in their simmering romance an outlet for her grief, artistic frustration and fears of inadequacy in her marriage to an overachiever. The nested stories of Marta and Celia—delivered as notes to epic phone conversations, and intimate monologues in the kitchen— capture the oral systems of information-sharing and storytelling passed among women throughout history. . . . [Burnham's] descriptions of São Paulo's neighborhoods, the rural town of Ati-

baia and the beaches of Trindade bring the reader into sensory contact with the setting. As well, her descriptions of the domestic sphere show us the subtle power dynamics at play there. Clear and intricate prose delivers such fresh phrases as 'slick like a peeled plum boiled in sugar water.' This is a remarkable story of secrecy, discovery and self-expression, delivered by a skillful observer."
                                        —*The New York Times Book Review*

"Set in São Paulo, this stunning debut centers on two women—one an American dealing with her recent transplanting to Brazil, the other a Brazilian maid reckoning with cultural views on race—who find themselves thrust together."   —*Bustle*

"The psychological thriller takes you on [the characters'] entwined journeys of uprootedness, history, class, privilege, sexuality and more."   —*Newsweek*

"This surprising debut centers women from differing backgrounds but who are bound together by need, memory and compassion. Themes of race, sexuality, gender, class and power are expertly interwoven in this engaging and insightful story of (in)stability, meaning-making and care."   —*Ms. Magazine*

"Burnham's exquisite prose [makes] Linda's shrewd observations lush and alive. . . . The writing veers from dreamlike to brutal and unflinching. . . . Linda's soul-searching is made compelling through Burnham's lyricism."   —*USA Today*

"I would recommend this book based on the cover alone. Thankfully, the story inside is equally gorgeous, following three women in São Paulo: the anxious and listless Linda; her conflicted but steady maid, Marta; and Celia, an intoxicating artist with whom Linda leaves home. A lush depiction of privilege and power, sex and stability, *It Is Wood, It Is Stone* is an elegant arrival of a new talent."
                                                          —*Elle*

"An absorbing and remarkably assured debut, *It Is Wood, It Is Stone* marries taut, cinematic suspense with intimate, textured domestic realism. . . . Hits a major refresh button on the genre of psychological thriller and gives us something immensely satisfying and new." —JORDY ROSENBERG, author of *Confessions of the Fox*

"A fever dream of a book, absolutely captivating and wonderfully destabilizing . . . I could not put it down. It is about uprootedness, class and color, and sex. It is about women on the verge—of collapse, of escape, of self-knowledge—failing and flailing and propping one another up. It is a book about the limits of propriety and the boundlessness of grace. Burnham is a writer of such remarkable insight, it's impossible to believe this is her debut." —JUSTIN TORRES, author of *We the Animals*

It Is Wood,
It Is Stone

A NOVEL

Gabriella Burnham

ONE WORLD
NEW YORK

It Is Wood, It Is Stone is a work of fiction. Names, characters, places, and incidents are the products of the author's imagination or are used fictitiously. Any resemblance to actual events, locales, or persons, living or dead, is entirely coincidental.

2021 One World Trade Paperback Edition

Copyright © 2020 by Gabriella Burnham

Published in the United States by One World, an imprint of Random House, a division of Penguin Random House LLC, New York.

ONE WORLD and colophon are registered trademarks of Penguin Random House LLC.

Originally published in hardcover in the United States by One World, an imprint of Random House, a division of Penguin Random House LLC, in 2020.

LIBRARY OF CONGRESS CATALOGING-IN-PUBLICATION DATA
Names: Burnham, Gabriella, author.
Title: It is wood, it is stone: a novel / Gabriella Burnham.
Description: First edition. | New York: One World, [2020]
Identifiers: LCCN 2020003905 (print) | LCCN 2020003906 (ebook) | ISBN 9781984855855 (trade paperback) | ISBN 9780593230220 (acid-free paper) | ISBN 9781984855848 (ebook)
Classification: LCC PS3602.U76377 I8 2020 (print) | LCC PS3602.U76377 (ebook) | DDC 813/.6—dc23
LC record available at https://lccn.loc.gov/2020003905
LC ebook record available at https://lccn.loc.gov/2020003906

Printed in the United States of America on acid-free paper

oneworldlit.com
randomhousebooks.com

987654321

Book design by Caroline Cunningham

Title page illustration by Michael Morris via composite images: Bridgeman Images/Two Suriname Snakes (snake); Getty Images/vladru (bathtub); Getty Images/Yayasya, Katerina Sisperova (bubbles)

For Anna

It Is Wood,

It Is Stone

Chapter One

I can still hear your words, the vibrant joy in your voice, as we sat in the back of a taxi stopped in traffic, the windows rolled down but no breeze blowing in, except for the occasional wind from a motorcyclist weaving past.

"Is it what you expected?" You clutched my hand and shook it with excitement.

"Maybe I should answer that once we've left the airport road. Don't you think?"

"I can't believe we're here," you said, not to me, but to a child waving to us from an adjacent car window.

The traffic sprawled for hours, barely moving, like a snake that had swallowed a calf. You had told me before that São Paulo was not the tropical paradise on postcards; it wasn't the pictures of women on the beach with fruit baskets on their heads. High-rise buildings traced the horizon and favelas extended for miles on both sides of the highway. We passed a road that broke into the dense favela tessellation, revealing clotheslines strung from brick wall to metal roof, and a young girl pushing a shopping cart filled with cans and palm leaves.

A barefoot man standing on the partition walked in front of our stopped taxi and began to juggle oranges for money.

"Look," you said and nudged my arm, but the cabdriver wasn't, so I didn't want to.

When the traffic moved again, just three car lengths, the man wouldn't step away, so the driver whistled and waved his arm out the window. Not angry, but persistent.

"Linda—give him some money," you said.

"I only have U.S. dollars," I said, stirring the contents of my purse.

You took out your wallet.

"They gave me fifties at the money exchange."

For a moment I saw you weigh whether you should part with a fifty-real note. Then the man moved to the side and the taxi lurched forward.

This trip felt like a series of fever dreams from the start. Just four months earlier, on a cold afternoon in September, you came home and told me you had something to tell me. The University of São Paulo had offered you a yearlong teaching residency in their history department. What you didn't know was I had spent that morning cleaning our home, weighing the something that I had to tell you, too. I'd been thinking a lot about an escape from Hartford. What would it be like to spread both my arms into thin mountain air, to have my feet planted firmly on the ocean floor? I thought about how faucet water might taste in Italy while showering our neglected garden, which, despite my best attempts, had browned long ago. I thought about our seven years of marriage, gathered the para-doxical concerns that had been plaguing me for the past several months:

I had lost my job.

I didn't have my own money.

All of our friends were your friends from the university.

I had spent the last year caring for my dying father.

Now my days were replaced with memories of everything I no longer had.

Because of these reasons, I thought that maybe it would be better for the both of us if I packed my bags and left for a while. I anticipated you might point out that these were all the reasons I should stay. Leaving you was less a solution and more like a heartbeat trying to break free from its rib cage. I couldn't go on like this, but knew I might not survive without you. And so I stood at our kitchen island, cutting a bundle of store-bought cilantro with a pair of scissors, waiting for you to come home.

I remember the sounds of the door cracking and closing, your shoes bristling against the doormat. You rushed into the kitchen and dropped a stack of papers next to the cutting board, blowing the cilantro onto the floor.

"Baby," you said, leaning over to help gather the fallen herbs. "I have got incredible news."

"Okay," I said. "But can you get the broom as well?"

"Forget about the cilantro. Linda—we're going to Brazil."

I knew you meant to state this as a proposition, not a declaration (the fact that you hadn't turned into a back-and-forth that neither of us want to relive). I write about it now only to show how excited you were, convinced that a year in São Paulo would be a transformative change. You told me I could take as much time as I needed to respond, but really, we didn't have that long. We would be leaving in early January, before the start of the Brazilian academic year.

An hour into our taxi ride from Guarulhos Airport, we arrived in our new neighborhood, Moema. There we discovered a district of mansions and luxe buildings. The trees grew unbridled from the sidewalks, cracking the cement, carpeting the ground with purple petals. I tried to imagine what São Paulo looked like before the concrete arrived. Swampy and mountainous, chirring with insects, the lush, viscous leaves bending like boat hulls. The São Paulo we saw stacked unrestrained in all directions, east to west, south to north. Outside our apartment building was a dusty inroad of gas stations and construction. When I stood from the taxi and stretched my legs, taking in our new environment, I could see, just beyond the urban moat surrounding our home, a mass of green. It was the entrance to Ibirapuera Park. The park was a manicured jungle, with palm trees that dangled strings of green coconuts and a pond where couples reclined to watch fountains spray and dance on the surface.

We dragged our suitcases into the lobby and stumbled into all of our boxes, the ones we'd shipped from Hartford the week before, organized in stacks against the wall.

"We forgot to list the apartment number," you said, and then looked at the elevator, which fit three people and a large bag of groceries if one person leaned against the door.

After ten or eleven trips, up and down, down and up to the fourteenth floor, we had all of our belongings inside. I barely noticed what the apartment looked like, just that our bedroom had a mattress and a ceiling fan. We peeled off our clothes, wet from the summer's humidity, and you rested your hand lovingly against my back, until even that was too hot and we spread to the opposite sides of the mattress. We fell asleep as soon as we shut our eyes.

I took a week to contemplate our move to Brazil, to give you a final answer. I didn't know much about São Paulo, other than the stories you had told me from when you studied there as a teenager. It sounded thrilling, lively, a place where you had grown into a young adult. I considered that maybe I too could evolve there, just as you had. I was surrounded by old wooden furniture we inherited from my father, heavy and chipped at the edges. His dresser, a grandfather clock, an army chest emblazoned with REAGAN/BUSH '84 and BUSH/CHENEY 2000 bumper stickers. He left us a bookshelf that housed only two books: a twelve-step program guide and a biography of Dwight D. Eisenhower. Most of this furniture he acquired from VFW garage sales and police auctions; it had no sentimental value to him, and yet, as much as it tormented me to be confined by it all, I couldn't bring myself to let it go. Leaving it behind felt like the only option. We could leave it behind and go to Brazil, and I wouldn't have to leave you too. I wouldn't even have to tell you that I had planned on leaving you.

I woke you up the following Monday before your alarm went off.

"All right," I said, gripping your bare shoulder. "Let's go."

"Really?" You rubbed your eyes. "Are you sure?"

And then the alarm began to sound. I pulled the covers over my head until your sleepy hand found the snooze button.

I woke up from our post-flight nap around three, in our new apartment in Moema, panicked. It took a few blinks of my eyes to register where I was—all I saw were the bare walls, whirling fan, and the damp sheets where you no longer lay. Even after my mind compiled the pieces and located my body in space— here, São Paulo, Brazil, and you, probably in the kitchen—the dread remained. It expanded inside my chest cavity. Mornings in our bedroom back home floated in front of my eyes. Dust particles hovering in the rays of sunlight. Each morning I would inspect my terrarium on the windowsill, the only plants I managed to keep alive, pink and green succulents and a leafy fern. I fussed over them adoringly, misting their leaves, picking off the dead bits, and reorganizing the stems so that they didn't block one another's light. My face began to tense and prickle, a sure indication that tears would follow, and they did—two streams in the corners of my eyes that crossed over my ears and fell to the pillow.

But then I thought of you, somewhere nearby, and how thrilled you were in the taxi, scratching your newly grown beard, endlessly observing the billboards and graffiti we passed.

"Dennis?" I called.

"I'm in the kitchen!" I heard you say, and for a moment I calmed, feeling like we could have been anywhere. When I found you in the kitchen, you hadn't opened any of the boxes, but you had discovered a bag of white rice and canned beans in the cabinet. I stood close to you as you stirred beans on the stove.

"Sustenance," you said, and revealed the bottle of cachaça we'd bought at duty free.

"Already?"

"Come on," you said, and tore open a box labeled DISHES, CUPS. You unwrapped two coffee mugs. "It's a celebration!"

In the evening we tried to make love on the mattress—you thumbed at my bra clasp, clumsily kissing my neck while I raised my arms in the air—but I was too tipsy to keep balance and collapsed on the bed. We gave up and went to sleep in our clothes.

The heat woke me early. I prodded my way through the kitchen and nuked the leftover rice and beans. The tiles felt cool on the soles of my feet and I imagined spreading my entire body, star-shaped and naked, to temper the heat. You woke soon after and spooned bean-stained rice, chewing as you unpacked kitchen items, seemingly unaffected by your hangover.

Marta would arrive the following day, while you were checking in at the university, filling out paperwork. I knew having a maid meant that cooking and cleaning, the things I usually took care of in our home, would go to her. But I didn't fully appreciate that she would be there, physically, another person in the apartment, every day. I wish I'd breathed more deeply into our aloneness that day, huddled together in the empty space, before you became mired with obligation, and before Marta, the apartment, and I became one.

I stood and walked to the living room windows with my bowl of rice and beans in hand. You came too, held me by the waist, and we looked outside at the canopy of beige and brown buildings, the Ginásio do Ibirapuera stadium across the street, and beyond that two water fountains jutting from the pond in the park. The pink morning sky hovered just above the buildings, as if the city had somehow been raised to the clouds, or the clouds lowered to it. We cracked the windows and kept the ceiling fan spinning, the ambient drill a background hum that we would, in time, unhear.

Chapter Two

The first time I met Marta she walked like she had water in her shoes. Her niece had opened a beauty salon in Atibaia, the town where she lived, and cut her toenails too short. I remember how raw they looked, wedged in her sandals, each nail painted blue with a gold star.

You had left early that morning to fill out paperwork at the university before classes began in a couple of weeks. You asked me to come with you, but I was eager to meet Marta. Technically she wasn't supposed to come until school was in session, but she had called ahead to say she would stop by to ensure everything was in order for us.

When she arrived, she knocked twice at the back door as a forewarning, then let herself in. For some reason I had the impression that Marta was an older woman by the way the Provost had described her, someone old-fashioned and stately, but Marta looked more like a rebel aunt than a wise grandma. She penciled her eyebrows into high arches that rose to her hairline when she spoke. Her sleeves were rolled all the way to her shoulders, revealing plump, toned arms and a weathered tattoo of a black star on her bicep, a symbol for her Ghanaian ancestors, she told me.

I held out my hand.

"I'm Linda," I said.

"Bom dia, Linda. I'm Marta." She cupped my hand in both of hers and, instead of shaking it, settled for a moment, like a hen incubating an egg. "Can you help me? I have lost something important."

She was looking for the spare key to the walk-in closet in the back of the laundry room, a space that was reserved for her. She ate meals and stored her personal belongings there. Normally it was in the drawer under the microwave, she said, but it had gone missing.

"It is a small gold key with a piece of green tape on the end. Did you see it?"

I hadn't, and so we embarked on a hunt to look for it. We rifled through drawers and cabinets, shook out the rugs, lifted our boxes and, when that turned up nothing, opened them to search through the books and photographs we had packed, as though the key could have slipped inside. It felt strangely thrilling to search with her, like she had instantly seen me as someone who had a particular knack for finding things. So it was disappointing, sharply so, when it was she, not I, who found the key. I was sure I'd be the one to find it.

"Aqui!" she said and revealed a small gold key on top of a jar of dried beans. "Here it is."

"Oh," I said. "And you're sure that's the one?"

"Yes. Olha." She pointed to the green tape. "This is the one."

And with that, she walked away. She headed straight for the closet, unlocked it, closed the door, and disappeared. I wasn't sure if I was meant to wait for her, so I slinked into the living room and pretended to busy myself with a stack of books you had left on the coffee table.

When Marta emerged she was wearing a purple apron with ladybugs embroidered along the hem. She used this apron like a tool kit; inside was a bamboo toothbrush, a small Swiss Army knife, a cloth handkerchief, and a fan that she unfurled when she was hot, revealing a lily garden and a koi fish pond.

"Do you want me to show you the apartment?" she said.

I said I did, and followed her into the bedroom.

The welcome package had emphasized the historical importance of the apartment. It was situated in the center of São Paulo with many desirable landmarks. Renowned professors, like you, had resided there over the course of thirty years. Before we arrived, I had imagined a palatial estate, modern and new, the kind of place that would ruin whatever previous notion I had of luxury. Rather than regal, though, the apartment was manageable. It looked lived-in, with sun-bleached carpets and a sagging sofa, scuffed doorknobs and browned light switches. It was clear that we weren't the first to stay there and we wouldn't be the last.

Marta's manner made this even more apparent. She moved swiftly through each room with the ease of someone who is comfortably at home. She kept a trash bin next to the sink, about the size of a gingerbread house, which she emptied into a large metal can in the laundry room. She used a squeegee to wipe excess water around the sink. Don't hang damp towels on the door, she warned me. Hang them on the bar or else they'll never dry with the humidity. Toilet paper goes in the bin, not in the toilet (a mistake we would make for weeks before we learned). Keep the water canteen three quarters of the way full; it leaks if it's filled to the brim. The vacuum has a sucking problem—it doesn't work on the linoleum floors or the straw rug in the living room, only on the carpet in the bedroom.

The tour finished in the kitchen. Marta untied her apron and announced she needed to leave.

"Can I make you a coffee first? I boiled water before you arrived."

She said she had a bus to catch in an hour.

"Please, let me make you a coffee," I said again, already pouring the sputtering teakettle over the grounds. "As a thank-you for the tour. It will only be a few minutes."

She agreed to a few more minutes, and sat down on the edge of the chair, half on, half off, watching as she flexed her toes against her sandals. I would come to learn that it was rare for Marta to sit. She was always moving—she hardly ever lingered. Only once did I see her stop to peer out the living room windows to catch a sunset falling behind the stucco-and-glass cityscape.

I handed Marta a coffee with warm milk. She took a small sip and smiled.

"You don't like it?" I asked.

"It's delicious. American coffee is like this—weak."

She stood and pulled a jar of instant Folgers from the back of a cabinet.

"You won't be offended if . . ." But before I could tell her no, I wouldn't be offended, she had spooned two tablespoons into her cup.

I would have liked to believe that once Marta and I sat face-to-face, woman to woman, the imprints of housekeeper and kept woman would dissipate into the coffee. If only I knew how little I knew. Marta and I didn't talk about her, or me, or what she did, or what I did, or what she loved, or what I loved, like two old pals gathering for an afternoon tête-à-tête. We talked mostly about you. It was our point of communion, the reason why we were both there.

"What does he teach?" she asked.

"United States history," I said.

I explained that you were the youngest professor to be

awarded this residency. You had published a paper that garnered a lot of attention in certain academic circles, and the Provost was a lauded member of these circles. She asked what the paper was about. I told her I hadn't finished reading it. You had given it to me in starts and stops while you were drafting—half an introduction, a sentence or two read aloud before bed. But when it was eventually published, I never sat to read it in its entirety. Part of me felt more comfortable relating to the process than interpreting the finished product. I knew it was about a slave revolt aboard a whaling ship from New Bedford, one you had been researching for years. After the Provost read the paper and learned that you were fluent in Portuguese, and, better yet, that your grandfather was from Portugal, he called you directly to invite you to teach.

"How impressive," she said. "Do you have children?"

"Children?" I forced a chuckle. "No."

"Why not?"

"Well, certain things have to happen for—" I stopped, startled by the idea that I might talk about our sex life with Marta. I gulped down my coffee. A murky lake of grounds and milk sat at the bottom of my mug. "Do you?"

"No." She pressed her hand against her stomach.

"Not everyone needs children," I said, at which point she gladly changed the topic.

"Is it very cold where you are from?"

"It is. But it's almost spring there."

"Better you are here then," she said. "Where it is warm."

"I actually like the cold." I thought of the iced-over cliffs on the side of the highway. I thought of the time a red fox dashed across the snow in our backyard. "Have you worked in this apartment for a long time?"

She paused as if to calculate, though I sensed she kept this number on the tip of her tongue.

"Next month it will be thirteen years."

She stood and slung her purse over her shoulder. "Desculpa, Linda, but I should leave. My bus home is in thirty minutes."

I walked her to the door and thanked her.

We shook hands goodbye, which afterward felt too formally American.

And then she said, "You know, your name, Linda. In Portuguese, this means beautiful. *Leen-da*."

I thanked her by smiling forcefully, unsure how to respond, until she closed the door behind her, latching it shut with her key.

Chapter Three

When I first learned about Marta, I insisted that we didn't need her. What would we need a maid for? We were two people moving to an apartment for a year, two people who had spent our lives together without a maid. I didn't even have a job—how could I justify having a maid? And I could only imagine what Marta would think of me, "the Professor's Wife." Even the word, "maid," evoked images of the Gilded Age, with women in pastel lace petticoats who couldn't fart without a servant holding up their skirts.

"That doesn't sound like us," I said. "Since when does having a maid sound like us?"

We were sitting on the blue sofa in our living room in Hartford, reading through the paperwork the university had sent you.

"Actually, my family had a housekeeper growing up," you said.

"Really? I didn't know that."

"I never told you about Dottie?"

"No."

"She came once a week. We loved her. And then she moved back home and we never heard from her again." You looked down at the welcome packet splayed on the coffee table. "I almost forgot about Dottie."

"Well, I never had a maid. If anything, my parents gave birth to me so that I could be their maid."

We laughed, even though I was halfway serious.

"It's normal in Brazil. Everybody has one. It's not even an upper-class thing. The Provost said her union cleans many apartments in the neighborhood. Which, by the way, is a nice neighborhood. Did you see—"

"Does the maid have a maid?"

"You mean, do we get two maids?"

"You said everyone in Brazil has a maid. Does Marta have a maid to clean her home, or does she do it herself?"

"I don't know. You seem irritated by this."

"I'm not irritated. It's just"—I paused, searching for an explanation—"if Marta cleans our apartment and cooks our food, and you're at work, what am I going to do all day?"

Even as the words left my mouth, I heard how desperate they sounded, maybe even pathetic, and I wished I could collect them and shove them back inside. But it was an honest concern. The house had become a way for me to gauge my emotional health. How many days had it been since I made the bed? Did I have clean underwear in the drawer? Did we have more than alcohol and deli meat in the refrigerator? Giving these tasks to someone else felt, in a way, like taking away my walking cane when I couldn't see.

You pulled me into your chest.

"I'll ask the Provost for some information on her. Maybe it'll make you feel more comfortable. And then you can start to imagine all the things we'll do in São Paulo outside of our home."

The Provost sent an email with more information on Marta's background. She was the only English-speaking maid they could find, which made her "especially unique." She'd learned English by watching American television shows in the maid's quarters where her mother worked. Her mother had been a maid too. The university liked to use her for American or British professors who traveled there for residency. She had grown up cleaning houses, so her expertise was "unparalleled," he wrote.

"Maybe she'll want to split cooking with me," I said. "It might give her a nice break."

"Maybe. I'm sure you could talk to her about it."

"Like I could do lunch, and she can do dinner."

"She might be able to teach you some Brazilian dishes."

"That would be nice."

"See, there you go. It's not so bad."

I picked up the welcome package and flicked the pages against my thumb, watching the pagination race backward like a flip-book animation.

"It's not so bad. It might even be good."

Chapter Four

The night after I met Marta, in the middle of the night, I got up to use the bathroom. The air sagged with humidity. I could hear the last dregs of a party in the adjacent apartment echoing through the windows, which we kept wide open with the fan turned on high. A woman was singing Madonna's "Like a Virgin," but she only knew a few of the lyrics. *Like a virgin. Touched for the very first time.* I imagined the scene clearly: a snacked-over bowl of potato chips, edamame shells strewn on the glass coffee table, red-rimmed wineglasses and empty bottles, the woman, her lipstick faded and feet bare, unable to sleep, a song stuck in her head.

I thought of something Marta had told me earlier in the day, while she gave me her tour of the apartment. Her nephew had been the altar boy at mass. He wore a white-and-red robe, she said, and swung the thurible down the aisle, incense whirling behind him. When he got to the end, he turned and gave the crowd a thumbs-up, something she had taught him to do. She was so proud.

Your arm was splayed over your head, mouth agape with

slumber. The woman at the party broke something, a glass, and you stirred, rolled over to the other side, and snored softly. I watched you sleep from the bathroom doorway, your face slack and gentle, your arm reaching to my side of the mattress, while the woman swept glass and sang.

You're so fine. And you're mine.

Marta's nephew was seven years old and already studying English in school, which was around the same age Marta had begun to learn. He and Marta called English their secret language and would practice together in front of the family to demonstrate their special bond. Her sister had a small gathering at her house in the mountains of Atibaia, where they lived, to celebrate after church. Her nephew ate the biggest slice of chocolate cake. He wouldn't take off his altar robe, even for bed, which seemed to be Marta's favorite detail.

I sat on the toilet. It was one of those endless pees, the kind that comes and stops and comes and stops. I rested my elbows on my thighs and my head in my hands and looked toward the open window. There I noticed a strange thing happening. All the way up on the fourteenth floor, a thin green snake had found its way into our apartment. It was hanging off the ledge and searching for a grip on the tiles.

The woman was getting tired. I imagined her sitting upright in a chair, and every time she began to sleep she would tip forward, sing a lyric, then doze again. I was tired too. The snake wasn't a snake, I realized; it was more likely a millipede or a caterpillar. *With your heartbeat, next to mine.* It had crawled down the wall and was halfway across the floor. Marta's nephew and his older brother loved to collect dead caterpillars on the mountain trails, she told me, and save them in a shoe box that he kept next to his bed.

This snake-caterpillar-millipede charged toward the closed door. I watched, thinking, It's closed. You'll have to turn around and go back to the window. But the crack was just wide enough for it to slip under. I flushed the toilet and flung the door open. Where was it? I searched and searched in the glow of the bathroom light. It had disappeared.

After I fell back asleep, I dreamt that I was sweeping dirt into my own mouth and vagina while I lay like a doormat on the floor. I woke up suddenly, worried that no hole in my body was safe, that it would find a way inside.

Chapter Five

The morning you left for your first day of teaching at the university, I woke salty with sweat. Water thumped in the shower like dead piano keys, the faucet squeaked shut, you gargled, walked with wet feet across the tile floor. Everything moved in an anxious slow motion. Drawers opened and closed. The bedroom door shut. Pots clanked and the kettle whistled. In bed I waited for the sound of a closed door. Shuffle. Hitch. Lock. Silence.

I prodded my way to the bathroom and turned on the shower. Sunlight angled from the window to reflect quivering white diamonds around the glass stall. It took a bit of coaxing at first, going from hot air to frigid water. The chill hit me front-on, seized my lungs, and I swallowed deep gasps of air. After a few minutes, with my arms clasped tight, my body acclimated and the cold water began to feel warm. I pressed my fingers against my skin and watched the impressions turn from pink to white.

At thirty-four my body was still smooth, but no longer buoyant. My cheeks and belly were elastic, my breasts large and soft. I massaged the black bar of Phebo soap between my hands until suds ran down my arms, then rubbed it up and down my body, feeling for the prickly hair on my calves.

This small standing shower reminded me a lot of the shower we'd had in our first apartment in Boston. We'd both cram inside to shower together, alternating underneath the water stream, part of my body always touching yours. This was almost ten years ago, when I was twenty-five and working at a sporting goods store in the CambridgeSide Galleria mall. I wrote occasionally for zines, flyers, hotel brochures—anything to save me from minimum-wage doldrums. You were an academic with soft hands and a propensity for contemplation above everything else. It felt so easy to combine my life with that of a handsome PhD student at Harvard, who rode his bicycle down Comm Ave alongside the T. I would wave at you from the Green Line until we reached your bay-windowed apartment in Coolidge Corner. Once, we baked a whole roasted chicken with thyme and Maldon salt that you got from the alumni lounge. You played me bossa nova classics that your grandfather had played for you, and I read you a Frank O'Hara collection that was two months overdue at the library.

You convinced me to stop working at the mall after we had been dating for only three months. You said I was too talented, even though it was never a matter of talent but of necessity. That was our essential difference—you approached life as a series of strategic decisions, and each one led to the goals you had established as a young boy (comfort, prestige, money, intelligence, flexibility). I saw life as the unavoidable consequence of a system much larger than me. My goal was to find a wormhole, a channel to escape the odds, so that I too could achieve those things.

I guess, in a sense, you were my wormhole. We married under the gazebo in Provincetown that your father had built for your mother in 1978, carried away by your uncle's vintage Aston Martin. Your parents bought us an apartment in Boston, where I had my own desk and computer to write. I didn't have to work at the mall. You paid off my student loans. When my father got sick, you made it financially possible for us to move back to Hartford so that we could take care of him. These kinds of huge decisions were easy for you; you had the confidence that nothing was too big for you to accomplish—or buy.

It was this same confidence that drew so many people to you. I still sometimes wondered, even after all these years, how it was possible that you had chosen me. The fact that you had, unequivocally, made me feel both special and insecure. I imagined you inside the University of São Paulo with your new students. You wore your white linen suit and combed your hair to the side. I thought about the pretty young ones as they watched you in the halls. The young professor, with your nurturing smile. The students, eager for your attention. Did you ever look at their fey, supple bodies? How their necks and hips moved with natural elasticity? How they traveled in packs, the rest huddled behind while one emerged to ask you a question? Did you ever think about my body when admiring theirs, or theirs when admiring mine? Which did you find more attractive? I warmed my fingers inside my mouth and worked them between my legs.

But before I could finish I heard a loud noise from the other side of the wall. I turned the faucet off and stood, still naked and dripping. For a moment I thought perhaps you'd forgotten something. I pushed the bathroom door open half an inch, just enough to see a moving body fill the crack. Marta was bent over our bed tucking sheets into the corners. I closed the door and wrapped myself with a towel.

"Marta. I didn't know you were in the apartment," I said

through the flimsy wooden door. "How long have you been there?"

She turned on the vacuum.

"I didn't know you were in the apartment!" I shouted over the noise. "You're early!"

Still no answer. I opened the door and tiptoed my damp feet across the carpet to the dresser.

"Marta?"

She turned off the vacuum.

"Bom dia," she said. "I come at nine."

I found my hairbrush on the dresser and began slicking my hair back, looking for something to occupy my hands.

"Okay," I said. "Thank you for making the bed."

When she left for the kitchen, I lay facedown on the mattress and replayed the interaction again and again in my head (*You're early! I come at nine! Thank you! Goodbye!*) I flipped to the cold side, let the towel fall off, and watched the walls cocoon around me.

The room was so starkly white, even the slightest glimmer of sunlight bounced from surface to surface. I curled up and massaged my eyelids with the tips of my fingers. An early memory of my mother began to percolate inside me. As a small child, when I didn't want to be hugged, I begged not to be hugged, she would squeeze me until finally I gave in and hugged her back. I remembered that deep relief, the feeling that she hadn't let go. I don't know how long I had been lying naked, but I began to smell lunch cooking in the kitchen. I put on a dress and went to see if Marta needed help.

"No," she said. "It's okay. It will be ready soon."

I watched her cut up carrots and celery and put them in a small glass bowl. She was preparing ground beef lasagna, which I'd learn was her specialty dish. She also made ground beef kibi,

or ground beef patties with lime juice, or beef stew with pota-
toes, or ground beef pasta and tomato sauce sprinkled with
dried basil. Every afternoon she would wipe the table from
breakfast and put a plastic tablecloth down, a white one with
red flowers, and set a meal for me—a can of Guaraná, some
variation of a beef dish, vegetables, sometimes bonbons she
brought from home—then go to the closet in our laundry
room to watch novelas on her small television.

"Are you sure? I like to cook."

"No," she said. The knife hit the cutting board with metered
thuds. "Don't worry."

There were two bottles of tomato sauce and dried pasta on
the counter. Oil smoked in a skillet on the stove. She scraped
the raw meat off the wooden cutting board and into the pan. I
could see that a watery pool of blood had filled in the divots on
the cutting board.

"I don't want to impose." I spoke gently. "But maybe you
should use the plastic cutting board for raw meat."

She rested her chin on her left shoulder and formed a peculiar gesture with her hand, pressed her index finger and thumb
into a circle, and scratched her nose. She dropped another piece
of beef into the pan.

"Wood is fine for meat."

"Sure. It's not a big deal." I pointed to the cutting board.
"But you see. The juices seep into the wood." The mixture of
raw beef and humidity made my stomach turn.

She ripped a paper towel in half and sopped up the bloody
juice from the board. "I have always used wood. Wood has
been around much longer than plastic."

My mind inched forward and crawled through the blood-
soaked paper towel, the cutting board, Marta's hair tied loosely
over her shoulder. I imagined I'd have to pull a long black
strand from my mouth, feel it tugging through the bits of food

I'd already chewed. I swung nauseatingly between worry and disappointment in myself for being worried.

"Please," I tried again. "I'd really like to help."

From the look on her face, a face that was deeply settled into procedure, I didn't think she would let me. But then she handed me an onion, a plastic cutting board, and a knife, and asked me to chop it for the pasta sauce.

"Thank you," I told her and set up my station next to her.

It was a beautiful onion: perfectly round and white with a golden tuft of hair at the top. I peeled back the papery shell and admired the smooth inside, as shiny and lustrous as mother-of-pearl. I took the knife and pierced the onion at the root, as I'd learned from Julia Child's cookbook, but the knife was dull and it slipped, narrowly missing my thumb. I looked at Marta to see if she'd noticed, but she was standing at the stove stirring the pasta.

I let out an audible sigh. "I almost cut myself. This knife isn't very sharp." I waited for her reaction, but she didn't respond.

I looked for one of the knives I'd brought from home and found it tucked behind the silverware. The moment I cut into flesh, the onion's acidic spray was released into the air. The farther the blade sliced, the stronger the burn, and I could feel my eyes begin to pour. I cried, chopping and chopping, tears dripping from my chin, my eyes swollen. I turned the onion sideways and continued until half of it was rendered into small, seeping dices.

Marta heard me sniffle and handed me a towel. Her eyes sparkled with dryness.

"How are you bearing this?" I asked, blotting my face with the dishrag.

She shrugged and responded flatly, "Many years of cutting onions."

I left for the bathroom to rinse my face.

Many years, I thought. I looked in the mirror and watched beads of water splay across my sunburnt cheeks, the roots of my hair frizzed from the humidity, unsure which way to turn. I had envisioned Marta and me together whimsically in the kitchen, chopping herbs and taste-testing each other's sauces with a wooden spoon. I felt silly for believing that Marta and I would become instant friends, for having assumed that we would feel fundamentally connected, like an apprentice to her mentor. Maybe she thought I was feeble for almost cutting myself and crying over an onion. Why did I want her to feel sorry for me? I had felt a tug, just then, for her to stop what she was doing and acknowledge that I was in pain, that my eyes throbbed with tears, that I had been inches away from drawing blood. No, maybe it was that stupid comment I'd made about the cutting board. Why had I said that? I didn't actually care which cutting board she used. Or maybe she had heard me pleasuring myself behind the bathroom door? Did I moan out loud? A hot flash drew into my hands and feet and the tips of my cheeks.

I slinked back to the kitchen, ready to start again, when I saw that she had finished chopping the onion and had already stirred it into the pan.

"You're done?" I asked.

"Yes," she said. She took out her fan and waved it across her face; the baby hairs that framed her hairline blew majestically back. "Lunch will be ready soon."

Defeated, I left for the bedroom and shut the blinds. Marta never came to get me. Or maybe she did, but I wasn't awake. I lay on the bed to rest my swollen eyes and dreamt through the passing hours. The silence woke me. On the kitchen table she had left me a plate of pasta with beef covered with plastic wrap.

That night, you returned home with the flitting energy of an emptying helium balloon and began recounting your day as soon as you walked through the door. The bus ride had been busy, with people filling the aisle and the stairs from the front to back. You worried that you wouldn't be able to get off at the right time. But another young professor recognized your faculty tote bag and helped you push forward through the crowds. You described the students as organized and mannered and much more diligent than the wealthy students you'd taught at St. Gregory's. (Was it a matter of affluence, you wondered. Or stricter schooling? Or maybe you were projecting.) Your classroom was vast with large windows and glossy, round-lipped plants in every corner. The Provost had dropped in unexpectedly and introduced you in front of the class.

"He told them it was a privilege to have me join them," you said, your hands flailing. "A privilege!"

We went to the living room sofa and you stacked your feet on the coffee table.

"Anyway. Tell me about your day."

"It was good," I replied.

"Good?"

"Yes. It was good."

"Anything interesting happen?"

"Not really. I did some unpacking."

"How are things with Marta?"

"Good."

You turned to me.

"Good, huh?"

"Well, what do you want me to say? I didn't have as exciting a day as you. There's still a lot to do at the apartment."

You yawned.

"Did she cook dinner? I'm starving."

"It's in the refrigerator."

You heated pasta in the microwave and brought it back to the couch. I could smell the reheated meat, ripe like an old dish sponge, steaming from the bowl.

"This is delicious," you exclaimed and spooned faster than you could chew.

"I make that dish all the time at home."

You didn't answer. We sat for a few minutes as I listened to you clink the spoon against the bowl, filling your mouth with Marta's pasta.

"Can I tell you something?" I said.

"Of course."

"I get the sense that Marta doesn't like me very much."

You stopped chewing.

"Where'd you get that sense?"

"I tried to help her cook and she practically batted me away."

"It's her first day. You just need more time together."

"Do we? I mean, I know I've said this before but . . . do we even need her?"

You rolled your eyes and put down your empty bowl.

"You're the only woman I know who would complain about having a maid," you said. You then brought your dish to the kitchen, unbuttoning your dress shirt as you walked. When you returned I could see your chest hair darkened with perspiration. "I'm going to take a shower. Maybe try and think of all the ways it will be useful to have Marta around."

I listened to your feet pat against the shower tiles. The words, useful, Marta, useful, Marta, spun in my mind, until all I could hear were sounds with no meaning.

Chapter Six

For days I would sit in the kitchen over the course of an afternoon, reading, eating, sorting through papers, while Marta washed dishes, cooked, ironed, swept. You said she and I needed to spend more time together, and so that's what I set out to do. I tried to lure her into conversation with different entry points. I asked her opinion on Portuguese versus English, if she spent any free time in São Paulo, what her hometown was like. She answered me thoughtfully (it depended on what she was trying to express; she liked to go for walks through Ibirapuera; Atibaia was a humble town in the mountains), but these questions did not hook her for long. She was always concentrated on the pot she stirred, the shirt she folded, the dish she washed. She didn't do these tasks absentmindedly. I could see that there was an energy behind her brown eyes, the careful lines that formed at the corners of her lids and across her forehead, the way she held on to her hip with one hand. Marta retreated into a deep meditation as she cleaned and cooked; in an instant, as if by magic, she blocked all exterior noises and clamor to form a quiet, solitary bubble inside her mind. Occasionally she would ask me a question over her shoulder: How much coffee do you want? Will you eat dinner at home tonight? Who does this shirt belong to? I would respond, and then she would return to the inside. There wasn't much room for me.

It crossed my mind that maybe I should leave her alone. I could stay on one side of the apartment, she on the other. But even when we were separated, my thoughts would tiptoe out of my ear, through the kitchen, and next to her. What was she doing? Folding? Washing? What was she thinking about? I wondered if she wondered about me. Or did I escape her memory as soon as she walked out the door?

I read every travel brochure discarded in drawers around the apartment. I went for walks down Avenida Paulista, stopped at street vendors, and circled around sidewalk performances. I saw art exhibitions at MASP and Pinacoteca. I tasted strawberries at outdoor markets and photographed Beco do Batman graffiti murals. I spent several afternoons lounging on a blanket in Ibirapuera, watching a group of boys practice soccer, or trying to read a book, but I would glaze over the pages, wondering what you were teaching that day or what Marta was doing at the apartment. I saw every tourist site in a ten-mile radius, until I realized that experiencing São Paulo alone, guided by old tourism pamphlets, felt like observing the city through backward binoculars, distant and warped. Each day I tried to feel a part of the world around me, but more and more I felt like I had jumped into a well when I wanted to swim in the ocean. I wanted to feel involved, surrounded, woven through. At the very least, I wanted to have a small sense of purpose when I woke up in the morning.

And so I concocted a plan, whereby Marta and I would have separate but equal shares of the apartment duties. She would have hers, and I would have mine. I decided to run this idea by her while she was brushing her teeth at the laundry room sink, using the bamboo toothbrush she kept in her apron.

"Marta, how would you feel if we divided the cleaning and cooking?" I asked.

She responded inaudibly, her mouth full of toothpaste, and nodded, so I took that as an indication that I should show her what I meant, though somewhere in my mind I knew that I had purposefully asked her at a time when she couldn't really answer.

When I heard Marta close the door to her room, I went and found a large sheet of grid paper underneath the bureau. I drew a map. A large square in the middle for the living room. Below the living room, a smaller rectangle for the kitchen, and below that another square for the laundry room and Marta's room. To the right side of the living room I sketched a Tetris snake hall-way with two small squares for the bathroom and bedroom. HOME I wrote in big bubble letters at the top, then scribbled over and rewrote, OUR HOME, and then, even better, OUR TEM-PORARY HOME. I drew little pictures to represent the chores that belonged in each room and circled the ones that belonged to me. Marta's chores I enclosed with a square. I drew a circle around the spider plants in the living room and kitchen. I put a box around the dishes. The bathroom too—I carved a large box around the bathroom box, and circled the chicken and apple in the kitchen and wrote "Linda—Lunch." I would cook again.

That's all to say, the map looked quite beautiful by the time I'd finished, but Marta was not pleased.

"Why am I square?" She stood over me while I sat at the kitchen table. She had just come back out of her room wearing a denim dress with a white lace trim.

"I was already circle," I told her. "So I made you square."

She seemed apprehensive—hands on her hips, clucking her

tongue—and so I explained what each picture symbolized and how we could schedule the chores around different rectangles and squares. As I spoke, she took a damp sponge from the sink and began to scrub a few stray ink marks I had left on the table.

"Does that make sense?" I asked, and she nodded, but I sensed she wasn't paying attention. Once I finished, she went straight to the laundry room to hang her clothes and fold ours.

I hurried after her.

"Marta," I said, and pointed to the blue shirt I'd drawn with the circle around it. "I can do the laundry."

She had my underwear in her hands, a particularly ugly pair that was faded and worn, which she finished folding and then faced me, her eyebrows pointed.

"You want to fold the laundry?" She had one hand on the pile of clothing.

"Yes," I said and pointed again to the map.

Marta brushed past me and into the kitchen.

"Okay," she said. "Then can I do the dishes?" But before I could answer I heard the faucet squeal.

I had entered a fight over territory without realizing that Marta ruled the universe. The apartment had never been mine for the taking. I left the map out on the kitchen counter every night before bed so that Marta would see it as soon as she arrived in the morning. She didn't offer it a glance or a touch. And why would she? Her routines were hardwired into the floorboards, the rafters, the walls. There was no use in trying to make my own. She had been there long before us, and she would be there long after. Some days I would remind her about the division of labor I had proposed, like an old tired song bellowing from the jukebox, and she would politely nod and smile as though it were the first time she'd heard it. Then she would proceed to clean and cook faster than I could keep up.

Chapter Seven

"I think it would be good for you to go outside," you said and pulled some money out of your wallet. "Breathe some fresh air."

"I've been outside," I said, splayed on the bed. "There's nothing left for me out there."

"How about lunch?" You threw the money next to me. "Take yourself out."

"I don't want your money," I said, and rolled to face the window.

It had been days, possibly even weeks, since I'd gone outside. I couldn't let go of the apartment, even just for an afternoon, for fear that Marta might grow roots in our bedroom and reorganize the air so that I could no longer breathe. She had called that morning from a pay phone to say the buses were delayed because of the rain. I could hear the commotion in the background—the anxious stir of late commuters rumbling like a wasps' nest. She wouldn't be in until noon.

You left, and, in the silence of the apartment, I knew you were right. I needed to get out. The only problem was, I didn't have an umbrella. Somehow I'd remembered to pack a garlic press and an English copy of *Anna Karenina,* but I hadn't brought any rain gear with me. I found a pair of rubber sandals and a shower cap, one of those transparent plastic caps that come in hair dyeing kits, stuffed inside the side pocket of a suitcase. I riffled through the closet hanger by hanger searching for a suitable outfit. I didn't want to wear anything I owned. It all felt drab and old, already used. I emptied half my clothes onto the floor when your white linen suit appeared from the back of the closet. You had placed it there after your first day of school, I remember, because you were afraid that it would lose its dry-cleaned crease.

Initially I thought, Let me just try it on, and I did. The shoulders were too broad, the crotch too low, the sleeves and pants too long. It shouldn't have worked. But when I looked in the mirror, I was captivated. I rolled the sleeves and trousers to reveal the silk mustard lining. It was as though I'd grown a new nose and needed to touch my face to make sure it was real. I fitted the shower cap over my head, tucking my hair inside, and put fifty reais in my (your) pocket. I walked out the back door before I could begin to think of reasons why I shouldn't.

As I stood sheltered under the apartment entrance, the rain sprayed like the edge of a waterfall. So much water had collected in the streets, the gutters formed rivers that sent clumps of black leaves the size of small animals streaming down the current. I contemplated each step to the street, testing the slipperiness of the entry's brick path. It took only seconds before the suit was completely soaked through.

I was the only person walking on the sidewalk—others had huddled under awnings and gas station canopies waiting for the rain to stop. The safest route was upstream on Avenida Brigadeiro, away from the park. I saw a car attempt to drive up the hill, his tires spinning over the rushing rainwater, then turn around and go the opposite direction. But I kept walking, and walking, my feet squishing in the rubber sandals, until I decided to stop at a corner pub that advertised cold beer and soccer.

I've thought many times about how I should explain this part of my story to you. I could let it unfold as it did: that I found a seat in the middle of the bar. The wet linen got pressed between my thighs and a cool trickle slid down my spine. The place was empty, save for a table of four men drinking amber liquor and playing cards, and a woman in the corner sitting by herself.

I could tell you about the bartender, how he watched the soccer game on the television while mindlessly wiping the tiled bar. He was young, couldn't have been older than twenty, and wore a delicatessen hat that looked like an upside-down paper boat. When he turned to ask my order, I saw a momentary glimmer of confusion. I took off the shower cap and put it on the bar. He smiled.

"O que você quer?"

"Brahma," I said.

He brought me a large bottle in an ice bucket and a small plastic cup that was cracked with wear.

I could tell you about the men and their matching straw fedoras, or the soft rock music that whispered over the stereo, or the faint mix of fried yucca and damp fur that wafted through the air. Or I could skip all of that, as it's inconsequential compared to what I saw when I saw the woman, the one who was alone, like me, reading a book on the other side of the bar.

I could trace her features with one pencil stroke: a round face that curved into full lips, a proud nose, and her hair, a dark lioness of curls. She acknowledged me with a subtle glance up from her book and offered a wave. I waved back. It felt as though I had already studied her cheeks and the shape of her eyes. I had sculpted and resculpted her shoulders and the curves of her fingers. But how, if I hadn't seen her before? I couldn't explain it then, and I can't explain it now. I felt I already knew everything about her, as though I had imagined it all before.

I saw my own face reflected in the bar mirror between two liquor bottles: a strand of wet hair curled against my forehead; mascara smudged under my bottom eyelashes. I poured myself a glass of beer and drank it down, then went to the bathroom to clean up. When I returned, the woman had moved to the stool next to me.

"We need to catch up to them," she said and tilted her head toward the men. I could smell the mix of sharp vodka and sweet orange juice coming from her glass.

"I agree," I said.

She told me that her name was Celia. She said, "I'm Celia," and tucked her hair behind her ear as if to give me a better look. She was born in São Paulo, though she explained that this didn't fully answer my question "Where are you from?" She had lived in the backseats of cars, in hotels, in big houses, and in closets, in countries all over the world. She'd learned English in London, where she'd spent a few years stage acting.

"Where am I from?" she repeated back to me. "Really, my home is the theater."

The bartender came over to offer her a fresh cocktail napkin and a drink. She perched gently on her elbows, spread her eyes wide, and asked for two drinks: one for her and one for me. He melted away, then rematerialized with everything she'd asked for, plus a bowl of chips. Normally this kind of coquettishness would have made me uncomfortable. Even before you and I got married, I'd struggled to find the competitive femininity that my girlfriends possessed, the kind that got them to the front of a long line or a free drink at the bar. But with Celia, the display, her colorful dance, seemed less for the bartender and more for me.

"Do you live in this neighborhood?" I asked.

"No," she said. "I live in Perdizes."

She picked up my shower cap and stretched the elastic band over her head so that it looked a jellyfish bulb, iridescent and smooth, and her locks were the drifting tentacles.

"Nice hat. Is this an everyday look?"

"It's for the rain," I said without any intended irony. What would I say if she asked why I was wearing an ill-fitting suit?

She didn't ask. She took the drink the bartender had brought her and pressed the wet glass against her cheeks.

"Is this a regular bar for you?" I asked.

She looked at me, her skin wet with condensation, and forced a laugh.

"I don't normally drink before noon, if that's what you're asking. It's been a bad day."

I told her I would listen if she wanted me to.

"Okay," she said, and poured the vodka orange juice into her mouth, held it in her cheeks, then swallowed in one gulp. "But I have to warn you, it's not a happy story."

I told her I didn't expect her to make me happy.

"I was on my way home from a warehouse that's far south in the city. Santo André. We may use it for a play. I manage a theater company. Did I mention that?"

She sighed and asked the bartender for a splash more vodka, which she measured with two fingers.

"The bus I was on hit a boy. Actually, no. It wasn't the bus. He was holding on to the back of the bus while riding his skateboard. He moved out to the side, maybe to let go or change his grip, I don't know, and a car merged into the lane and drove over him."

"Shit. Did the driver stop?"

"The car did but the bus didn't. The driver mustn't have seen. I banged on the bus door, *Para! Para!* The other passengers yelled with me until the bus stopped. I got out. A few others left too. Cars had piled up. People were leaning out their windows, they were wailing, blowing their horns. A pool of blood—thick, brown blood—was leaking onto the pavement."

She dragged her fingers across the bar.

"Then the rain started. I didn't stay long enough to see the ambulances. I walked until I saw this bar and decided I would have a drink and dry off."

She examined my face for a reaction, then, perhaps in response to what she saw, eased off from the details.

"Maybe he's not dead. Maybe he's just hurt," she said.

"How old was he?"

"Fifteen? Sixteen? I didn't get a good look."

We waited for the bartender to offer another drink before we spoke again. He brought a Brahma that I told her we could share.

Then a thought intruded—an inappropriate thought, an untimely one, a thought that felt more like a memory. I saw Celia standing in our kitchen in Hartford. It was snowing outside and she was mixing batter to make pancakes with star fruit in the middle. Then I saw her in our bathtub, reading from my tattered copy of *Leaves of Grass*. My fingers dipped into the surface of the water.

Celia twitched with a hiccup.

"Can I give you a hug?" I asked.

Without saying anything, she wrapped her arms around me. I could feel the cold silk jacket lining press against my skin.

"Tell me," she said, letting go. "Why are you here?"

I looked at the raindrops collecting into shared streams on the window.

"To escape the rain," I said.

"Oh, no. I meant, why are you here"—she waved her arms in big circles around her—"in São Paulo."

"So you noticed I'm not from here."

"I had an idea."

"What gave it away?"

"I don't know. Maybe you look a little lost."

This made me smile. "My husband brought us here. He's teaching at USP."

"Ah. A professor."

I nodded.

"Are you a professor too?"

"No. I used to be a reporter. Now I'm just me, I suppose. In Brazil, trying to figure out what that means."

Celia stared into her drink for a moment and bobbed her head with recognition.

"I had always considered myself a writer. But is a writer still a writer if she doesn't write?" I trailed off, unsure of what I was trying to say. Celia laughed and repeated what I'd said, as though it were a riddle.

"Can I tell you something terrible?" I said.

She glanced at the men gathered in the corner of the bar.

"Claro."

"The day my husband, Dennis, told me he got this job in São Paulo, I was going to tell him I wanted to leave him."

"Wow." She pressed her hand against the bar. "You don't love him anymore?"

"I love him very much. Sometimes I wish it were that easy."

"Why isn't it that easy?"

"Dennis and I are shaped very differently. He has known his whole life what he wants. He is driven and the whole universe opens up to that drive."

"I see. I think I know Dennis. Not your Dennis. But I know who Dennis is."

"He's also loving, and loyal, and witty, and charming. When I met him, I didn't think it was possible that he could want me. I was working at a mall in Boston. My rent was only three hundred dollars and I could barely keep up." I took a sip of my drink. "I had never thought about what would make me happy. I thought constantly about how I was going to make money. Then Dennis appeared, and my life changed."

"Dennis gave you money."

"Yes. And he gave me love."

"So you didn't tell him you wanted to leave him?"

"No, I didn't. I thought maybe São Paulo would be a cure. A chance to reset."

She smiled. "Now you're sitting in a bar in Jardins, wearing a wet suit, drinking with a stranger. I understand the shape you've taken." She clinked her glass on mine. "I understand this shape."

"Maybe I made a mistake. I think I'm going mad. Like actually mad."

"Why is that?"

"I don't know where to physically put myself here. I don't know how to best use my time. I don't even know how to behave around Marta, our maid. It's like São Paulo is rejecting me, and so I'm rejecting myself."

"I would say two things to that. Don't give up on São Paulo. You've met me now. I'll show you the São Paulo you should see—not this sad bar in a rich neighborhood. And two, don't think madness can't cure you. I go mad all the time. Sometimes it's the only way out!"

I glanced over my shoulder and out the window. The rain had stopped.

"So you want to see me again?" I said.

She took out a pen from her purse and wrote her phone number on a cocktail napkin.

"Yes," she said, and shoved it into my jacket pocket.

I followed her lead, took out a napkin, and gave her my number too.

And then one of the men from the card circle came over and sidled up next to us. He swayed standing against the bar, his teeth yellowed, cheeks sallow, and gave us a wink.

"*Gataaaas,*" he said. The bartender was off somewhere sweeping the floor.

Celia turned her back to him, but her resistance enticed him even more. He cozied his hip against hers, purring and laughing.

"Tá bom," she said, firmly, but he mistook her protests for banter.

"Já chega," she said and, perhaps realizing that words alone weren't enough, she curled her top lip and hissssssed, baring her teeth at him.

His eyes widened, but he didn't leave, so she let out another HISSSSS, even louder and sharper, which sent him scurrying away to his friends. I saw that one of the men asked him what had happened, but he shook his head and said they should continue the game. Not to bother with us.

"I'm glad I met you," I said.

"You too," she said.

Celia was the one who said it was time for her to go. She worried that she would be too drunk to cook dinner and it was her night to feed her roommates. We walked to the curb and she reached inside my pocket to make sure her number was still there.

"Don't forget," she said, and stuffed it in my hand. Then she hopped into a taxi and sped off, her arm waving out the window.

The walk home sobered me up a bit. When I arrived, Marta had already come and gone, and you weren't back yet from school. I went to the bathroom and removed your suit. It had stiffened with dried rainwater. I brought it into the laundry room and considered how I might wash it without having to explain why it needed a wash. It wasn't dirty—you had just had it cleaned for your first day of school. In a jar on the windowsill there was a blue pen inscribed with the university insignia. Maybe I could scribble, just a line, and convince you it had happened while you were grading. Had you even been grading in this suit? I drew the line but it seemed too insignificant for a full wash. I drew another line, and then another, until eventually I snapped the pen in half and poured ink across the fabric, from the collar to the breast pocket. I drew a water bath and plunged it inside.

I do feel guilty, Dennis, but the suit had lived its full life that day. I couldn't bear the thought of seeing you wearing it for some meaningless conference.

Once I'd sopped up the ink in the soapy water, I took a warm shower, wrapped myself in a towel, and slept off the alcohol. You arrived a couple hours later. As soon as you walked through the door, I could see the dismay on your face.

"What happened?" I asked.

"It rained halfway through my walk to work. I spent the day soaking wet. A hurricane is coming up the coast. It's the first hurricane Brazil has ever seen. My students were panicked." You put your briefcase down on the kitchen table. "Is there anything to eat?"

I handed you a mango and told you I had bad news too.

"The white suit you love. I noticed a big blue stain, right above the breast pocket."

You pressed your hand to your forehead. This was your favorite suit, your most expensive suit, a gift from your uncle.

"There must have been a pen in the pocket," I continued. "And it broke. It's soaking in the back."

You rushed to the laundry room.

"It's ruined," you said, holding a sleeve out of the water bath. "What a shame."

I rubbed your back.

"Maybe Marta can fix it."

We agreed that we should ask Marta to try her hand at fixing the stain, so I left it in the sink until the following day. I brought her to the laundry room when she arrived in the morning.

"Dennis's suit has a little stain on it. Can you remove it?"

Because I'd left the fresh stain sitting in the water, the ink had diluted and absorbed into the rest of the jacket, dying the fabric a powder blue.

"Ai meu Deus," Marta said and wrung out the excess water. "I will fix it."

She stayed determined through the day, adding more detergent and scrubbing it against the washboard. But by the end of the afternoon, she had to admit defeat. There was nothing she could do.

"It's fine," I told her. "You tried."

Chapter Eight

I felt the overwhelming urge to paint. A levee had broken, and my mind filled with Celia. At first I didn't know it was her; at first she appeared as a burst of inspiration.

"I'm going to start painting," I declared. It was seven in the morning and you were getting ready for school.

"Oh yeah?" you said without any pants on, combing your wet hair in the mirror.

"Yeah. Do you know where I can buy paint supplies?"

"I don't. Maybe Marta knows."

I waited two more hours for Marta to arrive. She brought out an old phone book from a low cabinet and thumbed through the thin pages until she found an art supply store in Brooklin Novo. I took the subway and tried not to appear too obvious as I studied the map, memorizing how many stops until I had to get off. Two stops, I thought. Two stops. The young boy next to me listening to a Walkman, the woman across, carrying her daughter in one arm, a basket of groceries in the other, were all tired and quiet, unaware of my presence.

The store Marta had found was meant for children, I soon

learned. A bored clown looking for faces to paint greeted me at the door. Speaking in mime, he pulled me into a seat and began to decorate my cheek with a glittering butterfly. I was too confused to understand how to protest, but I liked the pressure he put on my collarbone to steady his painting hand. When he finished, a young store clerk helped me find the oil paint supplies. She filled my cart with everything she said I would need—paints, yes, but also an easel, canvases, linseed oil, large and small natural-hair brushes, sponges, a palette knife and a palette. She even called a taxi for me, since I was now adorned with too many bags to take the subway home, and waved sweetly from the entrance, the clown not far behind her. That's when I looked at the receipt and saw the price tag, nearly two hundred reais, and felt the twist in my throat that I had committed to more than an afternoon of leisure.

It started with an eleven-by-fourteen-inch canvas and a milky yellow coat. I set up my easel and a stool in the living room near the window. A strip of sunlight fell across my thighs. I waited for the coat to dry. Then I used pencil to sketch the outline of a face, just a face, that filled the frame. I had never painted before, never seriously, but it felt good to let my instincts lead the way. It took forever to get the size of the eyes right, the proportion, echoes of failed ovals enveloped each other, until finally I gave up perfection and dipped my brush. The oil paint pushed like soft clay on a riverbed—one minute it ran in a fluid stream, the next it was an embankment for another color washing in. The brush wasn't a vessel to transfer color so much as an instrument to contain, to manipulate, to stoke and calm. I finished the eleven-by-fourteen face and painted three more.

You walked in long after the sun had set. The only light on in the apartment faced my easel. You had undone the top button of your shirt and slung your tie around your neck like a sash.

"A butterfly," you said. The sudden sound of your voice startled me.

"I didn't hear you come in," I said and touched my cheek with the back of my hand. "Right. Yes. A clown at the paint store did it."

You placed your hand on my neck. It was cold and stiff, like you'd been writing on a chalkboard for too long. It made my shoulders tense.

"I won't ask about the clown," you said, amused. "What are you painting?"

Surrounding me were four canvas faces staring back at us, all at various stages of dry.

"I'm just practicing right now."

"Practicing? These look like more than just practice."

You began to reach for one, but I held on to your hand.

"Can we not just yet?" I said. "I don't feel ready."

You gave me a bothered look and pulled your tie from your neck, then shrugged and left for the kitchen to find the dinner that Marta had prepared. Potato and ghee soup.

Marta herself was very pleased, I think, that I had found a way to occupy my time so that she could occupy her own time as she pleased. When she arrived at the apartment in the morning, I was already settled in at my canvas, and would continue to be there until after she left for the day. I felt as though I had found a time portal within the canvas—a day passed with the same energy as fifteen minutes. Marta and I interacted only when she checked to see if I needed food, water, or coffee.

You and I, however, had not reached the same symmetry. The further I slipped into my painting world, the more curious you grew, as I had discovered something that didn't involve you, and this provoked your interest.

And what was it that I had found? For the first time in perhaps all my life, I had the space to explore my own thoughts without guilt or anxiety. As I constructed a woman on the canvas, visualizing her face in parts, memories entered my mind in flashes: the smell of my mother's travel-sized Dior perfume, which I wasn't allowed to touch; her taking me to see *All About Eve* at a vintage movie theater with red velvet curtains; the biting tug on my hairline as she gave me French braids. Slowly I was reconstructing a past that I had always neglected.

I remembered the first time I went to the beach. My father decided to bring our family to Cape Cod. The sun was deliriously hot and we'd forgotten the umbrella, which he couldn't make sense of. "I rested it against the trunk," he kept saying, and spent the day swatting away seagulls trying to steal the marshmallow–and–peanut butter sandwiches my mother had packed in tinfoil wrap.

I must have been about eleven, and I remember it was the first time I wore a bikini. I had growing thighs, new stretch marks, painful breasts. I'd found a pubic hair sprouting the week earlier. When I saw my father wasn't paying attention, I looked down at my body's transformation, now visible to the world, and pinched the inside of my arm to restrain the discomfort. My mother sat reclined on a beach chair, refusing to take her clothes off. She wore a pair of camouflage pants, an oversize T-shirt with Mickey Mouse on the front, and a floppy hat.

"I'm too skinny," she told me, and lit a cigarette.

Not even a year later, she met a rancher through a personal ad in the newspaper, divorced my dad, and moved to the ranch. Her body swelled, even her nose and the skin underneath her eyes, like she had been filled with something she didn't have before. She grew her hair out and wore it in a gray braid that swung between her shoulder blades. I spent my teenage years living with my father in Hartford. I saw my mother on alternating holidays, and every time we did see each other, we were each surprised by how much the other had changed.

. . .

One morning I woke up to find you standing in front of my easel, your face a few inches from one of my paintings, inspecting the woman reclined on a couch, her breasts conical and splayed to the sides. I recoiled.

"What are you doing?"

You turned and took a sip of your coffee.

"Just looking."

Then you gave the room a sweeping pass with your hand.

"These are incredible, Lin," you said and offered your assessment of each painting.

I stood silent in my pajamas. All I could think to say was thank you, then I moved closer to try to wedge distance between you and my work.

You pointed at a smaller canvas, one of the first faces I'd done, and took another sip of your coffee.

"Who is she?" you asked.

"Who is who?" I asked back.

"The woman in these paintings." You pointed to each, one by one, showing me the similarity in the hair and the eyes and the turn in her nose. "It's the same woman over and over again."

"Oh," I said, and leaned in closer to inspect them myself. That's when I saw what you saw—the lithe frame and full features, the wildness in her gaze. It was Celia. How had I not realized before? I felt my face flush and tried to conceal my embarrassment by covering my neck with my hands.

"It does look like the same woman." I frowned, pretending to be bemused, and told you I didn't know. I scrambled, plotted an escape. "I think I need some coffee," I said and boiled more water in the kitchen.

. . .

Once you'd made me aware that I had been unconsciously rendering Celia in my paintings, I felt increasingly that I was hiding in plain sight. I stacked the canvases with their backs facing out so that you couldn't look at them, then would steal glances at night after you'd gone to bed. I'd stop painting midstroke with the sensation that you or Marta was standing behind me. A few times I honestly thought I'd felt a breath blow against my shoulder and would turn to find no one there.

Your interest in my Celia paintings didn't wane. It was the first thing you'd ask when you got home from school. "How did painting go today?" Every time you asked, I felt the warm space inside me, open and tender from a day at the easel, begin to constrict.

"I'm making progress," I'd say, and you'd nod with approval.

You collected flyers from the university bulletin board advertising campus art contests.

"They're open to the public too," you hinted. You inquired about me auditing art history lectures and fine art classes. You brought me supplies I didn't need: elaborate measuring tools, organic cotton rags, and artisanal brush cleaners.

I couldn't distinguish between what was genuine support, and what was your competitiveness hidden behind enthusiasm. "Why can't you just leave it alone?" I wanted to say every time I saw you look at a half-finished painting. Your push to get my art into the world began to feel like a desire to expose me, like you didn't want painting to be precious and safe, that you wanted to make it public so I would flounder in a way you never had. I imagined the exposure would prove to you that you were comparatively better at your craft than I was at mine; that you had won the awards I was incapable of winning. But I didn't confront you, I couldn't, because there was a part of me that knew I was overreacting. Whenever I pictured the conversation in my mind, you appeared as an innocent cherub boy only wanting the best for me, and I appeared as a warted witch, lurching over my paintings, waving my cane at anyone who came near. Maybe you just wanted to help and I had taken you for granted. The multiple conflicting possibilities, the dialectic of it all, made the confusion even worse.

Painful memories began to surface as I painted, old, stupid fights we'd never resolved, and so they remained wedged in my hippocampus, incapable of loosening their grip. We were at the bank in Hartford. My mother had called me from Ohio earlier in the day, a rare occurrence, while I was at my father's. His health had noticeably declined since the previous week— his skin looked like the yellow underbelly of a snake—and he was refusing to eat the creamed corn I had made him at his request.

"Come on, Dad," I said and tried to shove the spoon in his mouth, more forcefully than I should have, and he began to cry from frustration.

Then my mother called. I had forgotten Mother's Day, she said. She told me that I cared about my father more than I cared about her, when she was the one who had looked after me when he was drunk. I hung up the phone, put my father to bed before the hospice nurse arrived, and left the creamed corn on the table. Then I picked you up and we went to the bank.

It was a Friday and I was depositing my last check from *The Courier* for an article I'd done on back-to-school fashion. I waited in line for a teller while you sat on the bench behind the partition.

"Next," said the teller.

I patted my back pocket, but my wallet was in my purse with you.

"Dennis—" I said and saw that you were now standing on the other side of the bank talking with Bruce and Genine Skinner, both of whom taught at St. Gregory's.

"One second," I said to the teller, who leaned back in her chair and waited for me to return.

As I approached, everyone turned toward me, smiling, and Genine said, "There she is!" in her usual passive candor.

"I was just telling them about how you're writing for *The Courier* now," you said.

Genine and Bruce were both grinning wildly, like two by-standers held captive, trying to signal to me with nonverbal cues.

"Oh, yes. That. It's keeping me busy." They smiled some more. "Dennis—I need my wallet."

Crossing the parking lot on our way to the car, I held you by the arm.

"Why did you tell Genine and Bruce that I'm writing for *The Courier*?"

"Because you are."

You sat in the passenger's seat and began fiddling with the radio.

"If they look for an article they're not going to find one. That was my last check, remember? They let me go."

You landed on a classic rock station and turned down the volume.

"They asked what you've been doing and I told them. Who cares about *The Courier*? You'll find another newspaper."

"I wish you'd just avoided the topic."

You turned your head to the window and pressed two fingers against your chin.

"How's your dad doing?" you asked.

"Not great. He's refusing to eat. And he cried again."

"I'll go check on him later today."

"Thank you," I said.

I thought you were going to say more, but you didn't, so I turned on the ignition and drove.

We didn't talk for the ten-minute trip home. When we pulled into the driveway you opened the door halfway and said, "I won't talk about your writing until you tell me I can," then went into the house.

You kept your promise. You didn't mention my writing again, and I never did find another newspaper. My father died a month later, and six months after that we were on our way to Brazil.

Chapter Nine

The Provost had been enthusiastic, if not emphatic, that we meet his wife for the first time at the Mercado Municipal. He described it as a cultural epicenter—where life in São Paulo happened. When we approached him and Melinda at the gray-stone entranceway, it was clear that they had been in an argument. The aftermath of bickering rested on their faces. Eduardo extended two arms and embraced you. Melinda gave you her hand, which you kissed (something I'd never seen you do before), and you introduced me as your wife, Linda, who didn't speak Portuguese but would try.

You kept telling me how much Melinda and I had in common. Melinda, the Provost's wife, the wealthy socialite, the Paulistana. I didn't see how that connected us, but you insisted. I think it had to do with the fact that we were both wives of historians, which meant that she too knew this particular isolation, when you left the present for the past, hundreds of years back, hundreds of pages back, with no return in sight.

"I think you'll understand each other," you kept saying.

"She's intelligent and very connected in São Paulo. She knows some fascinating people."

We both sensed that, between the two of them, Melinda had the money. Eduardo brought in a good salary as Provost, but not enough for a penthouse suite in Morumbi, a chalet in Saint-Malo, a vintage wine collection, and a library. Melinda exuded an overprescribed wealth, as though the world's sharpness had to be dulled just to manage the injustice. Why her and not the millions of others?

The first thing I noticed was her impatient, anxious energy, as though she was already late for a board meeting she needed to attend next, when in reality, she had nowhere else to be. She shifted her weight from one stiletto to the other, looked side to side, up and beyond.

We entered and you joined Eduardo ahead of us, while I stayed behind with Melinda, who walked with restraint. She lit a cigarette next to a fruit stand inside the market hall.

"Keep an eye on your purse, Linda," she said and adjusted my strap for me. "The pickpockets will rob you if you leave it hanging like that."

We followed you to various stands—cured meat hanging from chains, woven shoes and bags, large barrels of nuts and spices—but Melinda always stayed a few feet outside. She said it was because of her cigarette (she tapped one after the other from a soft pack in her purse), but I sensed that it had more to do with association. The entire building smelled like smoked cod and mandioca; not even her Chanel No. 5 could mask it. I asked her if she wanted to come outside with me for a change in scenery. It was the first time I saw her smile.

"I would like nothing more," she said.

I suggested we lean against the building, out of the way of the pedestrians hurrying down the sidewalk. She reminded me of a flower that had been pressed inside a book to preserve its beauty, so she had to present herself at an angle to mask her flatness. Maybe that's why it bothered me that you implied she and I had something in common. I always considered myself planted, not yet plucked.

"You're beautiful," she said, more like an accusation than a compliment. "You know your name, it means beautiful."

"Thanks," I said and twisted my hair over my shoulder. "I've heard that."

"This part of the city is very dirty," she said and squinted at the passing cars. "I'm sorry Eduardo brought us here."

Compared to Moema, the area outside the market was heavily traversed and wore a sooty sheen. But I didn't see any trash on the street, not even a gum wrapper accidentally dropped, like I had in U.S. cities.

"I'm happy we got to meet," I said. "Dennis really appreciates Eduardo and everything he's done for him."

"Eduardo loves Dennis." She looked over at the market entrance. "He is like a son."

She fumbled inside her purse, searching for the cigarette pack. When she pulled it out, I noticed a photograph of a stillborn infant on the back.

"Do you want one?" she offered.

"Sure," I said. "Why not."

She lit a flame for me, cupped inside her hands, and the two smoke streams converged in front of us.

"You are just the right amount of beautiful," she continued. "You're not so beautiful that you could make money from it. You're not a model. But you are beautiful enough that people will treat you well in restaurants and stores." She scanned my face. "You have good skin."

"I guess I've never had trouble in restaurants."

"I hope Dennis tells you you're beautiful."

The comment made me feel like I had to hurry to remember

the last time you did say it, which made me feel self-conscious, and then absurd. I took a drag.

"He does."

"My daughter is a model," she said. "She looks like me when I was her age."

"Does she live in São Paulo?"

"Milano," she said in a feigned Italian accent.

"You must miss her."

"She went to boarding school, then university in London, then Milano. I don't remember what it is like not to miss her."

Two children approached us with fistfuls of shell necklaces. The younger one held out her hand, offering them to us for fifty centavos, while her older sister spun behind her like a ballerina. Melinda bought a necklace and then shooed them away. Once far gone, the older sister threw a stone in our direction.

"Let's walk," she said. "If we stand here it will be like chocolate cake to a fly."

We walked for a few blocks, slowly, at Melinda's pace, and talked at length about her swim and yoga regimen. When the conversation reached a lull, she asked me about the apartment, if we had everything we needed, if the bed was comfortable, if we had enough towels and cutlery.

"Yes," I said. "We brought a lot with us from the U.S. We probably have too much."

"And how about Marta?" Her tone made me think that this was the question she had wanted to ask all along, and that her concern about bath towels was just a gateway.

"Marta? She's doing fine, I think."

"Is she treating you well?"

"Very well," I said. She waited for me to say more. "If anything, I wonder if I'm treating her well."

Melinda flicked her eyebrow. "What do you mean?"

The comment wasn't meant to mean much more than that.

I wondered if we were good hosts, but for some reason I found myself searching for a deeper explanation. The way Melinda framed her questions felt unobtrusively intrusive. She didn't ask much, but I felt I'd already given her too much.

"I didn't understand how this relationship worked, between her and me. How we were supposed to coexist. And so it was a little bit awkward at first."

"Awkward?"

"Yes, awkward. I've never had a maid before, I've never had to share household responsibilities, and so I thought maybe it would be helpful if I helped her. But she didn't seem to like that." I trailed off, worrying now that I'd opened a vulnerability for Melinda to prod. "But anyway, I started painting and now things are good. She doesn't have to worry about me meddling."

Melinda chuckled. "This is a funny concept. We pay her to make you feel comfortable. You're not getting paid to make her feel comfortable."

"No. No, that's not what I meant." I could feel my vocal cords tense; my voice dissolved into a low rasp. I cleared my throat. "I don't need to be paid to make her feel comfortable. Or anyone for that matter. I'm just not used to having her around yet. That's all."

"Don't feel bad," she said. "I'm not surprised you felt a little—what was the word you used?—awk-ward, when you first met Marta. She has a reputation for being quite an alpha for someone who works in a subservient position."

"I kind of like that about Marta."

Melinda shook her head as if she was exasperated by this. I thought, Don't argue with her. It's not worth the energy. Melinda was leading me down a precarious path, a conversation I would look back on with chilly humiliation. I was at the same time aware that you admired the Provost and his wife—in many ways, they held the ultimate power over your reputation as a professor. With the flick of a wrist, he could send you back to the United States with a scarlet letter emblazoned on your résumé. I couldn't combat her. I reached inside my purse and pressed my finger against the sharp edge of one of my keys to try to contain my discomfort.

"She is too brave," she continued. "Too brave for the world she's been built in. It would be better for her to adapt, for her own good."

I inched away from Melinda and closer to the road. The idea that you saw some of her in me, or me in her, made me retch. Her rant about Marta wouldn't stop. She told me about a visiting neurologist from Nice who thought that Marta oversalted the food. Coming from a Frenchman, Melinda said, this was surprising, but he swore that he could taste quinine in the salt. He preferred the salt on the coast of France. Then one day, in the middle of a lecture, he fell forward from pain in his abdomen. Two of the larger students carried him to the men's room, and he vomited into the toilet until a car arrived to take him to the apartment. While he was bedridden, Marta fed him soup until he got better. From that point on, all he had a taste for was Marta's food. He asked for all of her recipes before he returned to France.

"I'm not sure I follow," I said. "It sounds like he got sick and Marta helped him."

"Sure. When I first heard the story, I felt it was innocent too." She threw her cigarette into the street. "But then how do you explain the others?"

She told other accounts. The Dutch veterinarian who developed a rash across her entire body, which was eventually linked to the starch Marta used in her underwear. The English psychologist who fell in the bathroom after Marta mopped the floor. The German chemist who nearly broke his back from a spring that burst through the top of the brand-new mattress.

"Don't you think it's curious?"

"It seems more like a coincidence than a conspiracy," I said.

"You're young. You still see the good in people." She stopped and looked at me directly. "Go look in her maid's quarters. I'm sure you'll find dolls in there with needles sticking out of their eyes."

When she said this, I heard a sharp ringing in my ear that blocked the drum of the traffic around us. I needed to go home and take a hot shower, then hide under our bedsheets. Ahead I could see we were only a few blocks from the Mercado Municipal. I wondered if I would be able to reach it without boiling over. Melinda droned on for the rest of the walk, and I folded into a narrow chasm, deep inside, until we found you and the Provost standing outside the mercado with grocery bags hanging from your arms.

"There they are," you said and embraced me. I whispered in your ear, *I can't believe you left me with her,* but you either didn't hear me or ignored the comment.

The Provost wanted to show me all the exotic fruits you'd purchased. He pulled out a papaya and held it to my nose, told me to smell the skin, which had a faint perfume but mostly smelled like nothing, and did the same with a fig, a mango, and a small pineapple.

"You won't find fruit like this anywhere else. Here." He handed me a bag filled with figs. "Take these. They will be the most delicious figs you have eaten."

"Obrigada," I said, and Melinda smiled.

"De nada!" she said. "You see, she's speaking Portuguese. She needs to spend more time with me."

"Linda, I want you and Dennis to come to dinner at our

apartment," said the Provost. "I am traveling for two weeks, but when I return."

You held a steady expression. I knew you wanted me to say yes.

"Sure," I said. "We'd enjoy that."

"What do you like to eat?" asked Melinda.

"Linda is tired of beef," you quickly chimed in. "Our maid cooks a lot of beef."

I was startled by how the words "our maid" came so easily out of your mouth.

"Whatever is easiest," I said, looking at you. "I don't mind beef."

The Provost's wife gripped my back.

"My dear. We will make sure there is chicken."

Chapter Ten

After my encounter with Melinda, I quickly became skeptical of your budding relationship with the Provost. It was clear that he had a special interest in you, but I also knew how easily you were mesmerized by authority. I told you that I couldn't stand Melinda, that her personality grated on me, that she was a racist, that she abused Marta. I didn't want to interact with her. You said that she and I didn't have to become friends, but asked if I could pretend to like her when we met with them socially. "For me," you said. I begrudgingly agreed.

I began to wake with my hands clenched. In the mornings I found them tucked underneath my chin, wrenching into themselves. I had seen infants sleep like this, with their soft, bulbous hands bundled together, except that my hands lacked the same fleshy cushion. After hours of pressing my nails into the creases in my palms, I would wake up aching and sore, barely able to extend my fingers.

"Look," I said, holding my palms out to display the red lines where my nails had dented the skin. I managed a laugh. "I'm punishing myself in my sleep."

You sighed. I could feel your breath blow against my wrists.

"Maybe cut your fingernails?"

I turned my hands over and looked at my nail beds. They were chewed down from years of nail biting; even the skin around the cuticles was dry and bitten.

"I barely have any. It's like I'm self-harming with a butter knife."

I did file down what little nails I had and moisturized them to try to dull the edges. It didn't work. Instead the nightmares started. I had a postapocalyptic dream where I found my mother crushed underneath a car. She cried out for me to help her, so I tried to lift the car with my bare hands, but I knew she wouldn't survive. I jerked awake with my hands in tight fists, digging into the wall behind our heads. A layer of skin on my knuckles had been pushed off like a white film, revealing a smooth pink layer underneath.

Sometimes the dreams were closer to memories, darker and darker than the memories that emerged while I was painting. I dreamt of things I tried to forget. I dreamt of an old college fling who, on a snowy morning in bed together, rolled on top of me while I was still asleep—I could barely breathe underneath his weight—and pushed inside me. I woke with tears in my eyes. I dreamt of the time my father, drunk and upset that I hadn't cleaned the house, flipped all the furniture upside down and wrote me a letter saying that he might never come home. I dreamt that I was falling into a ravine, that I was dangling by a wire, that I was alone, that you had left me. I woke and held on to your hand until I fell back asleep.

The issue with the nightmares was that they allowed the real pain in my hands to integrate seamlessly with the world playing out in my head. The digging and scratching didn't wake me up. I assumed I was in pain because of the knives I dreamt I was batting away or the glass I had fallen into. You woke me up when I woke you up with my tossing and turning, but that happened only after the scratching had already gone too far. In a matter of a couple weeks, I began to develop sticky red sores in my thumb creases. I couldn't use soap or shampoo without upsetting the open wounds. I held my hands under cold water for minutes until they numbed, and then let them air dry by the fan.

There were other remedies we tried. I'd seen mothers put mittens on babies who scratched their own faces at night, so I tried to wear oven mitts to sleep. Every morning I'd wake up with them flung across the floor and my fingers curled in victorious fervor. I practiced deep breathing before bed. I meditated when I woke up. I didn't touch a sip of alcohol. None of it helped.

The worst of it was, I couldn't paint anymore. That broke my heart more than it hurt my hands. Even if I did manage to pick up the brush and eke out a few strokes, one wrong bend and my knuckles would send a violent quake through my radius bone, forcing me to stop. Just breathe, I told myself. If it had only been the isolated pain, I believe I could have fought through it. I used to work through period cramps that left me in a ball on the bathroom floor. The mental exhaustion was the real culprit, the chronic interruptions, that caused me to unravel.

Because you were teaching most of the day, Marta suffered the worst of it. At one point a terrible thought struck me, like an arrow that had been shot from miles and miles away. I remembered the story that Melinda had recounted, the one about the professor from France who didn't like Marta's cooking and fell ill while teaching. Maybe it *was* Marta who had caused this turmoil in me, just as Melinda had suggested? I fretted about this possibility while at the bathroom sink trying to brush my hair and burst into tears out of pure frustration.

"Let me help you," I heard her say, and she reached for the brush.

"No!" I demanded. "Stop. I can do it."

I regretted immediately the tone I'd taken, the thoughts I was having, how cruel I was being to her. I regretted it all—the chore map, the tension about cooking, my insistence on taking up more and more space in the apartment. I had become frantic. I just wanted the pain to go away.

"I'm sorry, Marta," I said to her. "It's me. It's the pain. I shouldn't take it out on you."

She brushed it off like it was nothing. It seemed Marta preferred not to admit when I had hurt her.

It was only after the sores became infected that I decided to bandage my hands. I had been resisting the idea because I felt they needed to breathe air to heal. There was also something depressing about seeing bandages on my hands, like I was powerless over my own body, that made me reluctant. I was reminded of Sylvia Plath's poem "Lady Lazarus." A bandaged woman I would be.

> Peel off the napkin
> O my enemy.
> Do I terrify?—
>
> The nose, the eye pits, the full set of teeth?
> The sour breath
> Will vanish in a day.

I could do the left hand myself, but you had to wrap the right. The white gauze turned yellow and moistened against the tender spots. You tucked the bandage end between my knuckles and kissed the tops of my hands. The bandages did prevent me from scratching myself, though I still tried. I'd wake up with loose, frayed edges from where I'd tried to pry for skin. We broke a Popsicle stick in half and wedged the pieces into my palms to make it harder to clench my hands. For the most part I kept the bandages on all day, but sometimes I would take a peek at the damage, the dark purple and puckering wounds. It gave me a strange thrill to see the ugly progress, to know the more disgusting it looked, the better I was doing.

I hadn't anticipated the new batch of pain that came with healing. The itch, the unbearable itch, that traveled underneath the bandages. I thought I'd known healing until I learned the pain of healing. The itch was so unbearable I had to rub the bandages against my legs for relief. Then one evening, I decided that I would take them off and let my hands breathe for the night, that maybe I wouldn't need them to sleep anymore.

"I'm going to sleep with the bandages off," I told you, lying on the mattress with my palms facing the ceiling fan.

You gave me a suspicious look and switched off the light. Hours later, you nudged me awake.

"Linda," you said. "You're shaking."

The moment I opened my eyes, pain flashed into my hands. I opened my palms. "I think I'm bleeding."

It was true. I had broken skin on my left hand. The blood started in the meatiest part of my thumb, ran into the creases of my palm and down my wrist. You led me to the bathroom and rinsed off the blood with water, which was alarming and roused so much feeling I had to cry. You didn't say anything, just wrapped my hands in gauze, gave me a hug, and led me back into bed.

You asked Marta if she would watch me, to make sure I didn't take off the bandages while you were gone, a precaution that was probably unnecessary while I was awake, but that Marta took very seriously. She watched me as though I would disintegrate if she looked away for too long. She made me bone broth soup and offered to hold the spoon for me after I dropped it on the floor from the soreness. I felt embarrassed having to rely on Marta so much, especially considering my testy mood, but this transference of care, me giving in to her, her allowing me to give in, opened up a sense of trust between us.

"Do you want water?" she asked, already handing me a glass. "You should drink more water."

I asked for ice and she let me have some, even though she was convinced that ice caused pneumonia. I took a sip. The cool liquid traveled from my head to my feet, numbing every part of me.

"How do you feel?" she asked.

"Better," I said. "I just wish I could paint again."

She fluffed a batch of white rice she'd made and spooned it into a bowl.

"Don't worry. You will paint again."

That night, I slept more soundly than I had since we'd moved to São Paulo. When I woke I wandered to the kitchen in a blissful haze, the corners of my mouth dewy and smiling, my eyes glimmering with rest.

"I slept!" I announced to nobody. You had been at school for hours and Marta was in the other room folding laundry.

I looked around the kitchen and planted myself more firmly into consciousness. That's when I noticed the wall. Not the wall, exactly, but what had been hung on the wall: a five-by-four-foot rendering I'd done of the woman who resembled Celia, lying in a bathtub, her face flushed pink, her breasts cresting from the turquoise water. My stomach fell to my knees.

"Marta?" I called. "Was this you?"

She appeared in the laundry room door.

"Yes. I thought it was a shame that they were all in a corner."

I didn't know what to say. My mind jumped through rings of shame. What if you ran into Celia on the street and recognized her from the painting? What if Celia somehow ended up in our kitchen and saw what I had done?

"I—" I began to stutter. "I—"

I felt my mind unclench.

"Thank you," I said. "Thank you for being so kind to me, Marta."

She smiled and began to walk away, but I went over to her and wrapped my arms around her, until she gave in and hugged me too.

Chapter Eleven

Celia finally called the day before we were meant to have dinner at the Provost's. I hadn't heard from her since we met, but I kept her phone number folded tight inside my purse and would check occasionally to make sure it was still there. I think there was a part of me that believed she wasn't real, that she had been an apparition I'd imagined, and if I called her and she didn't answer, it would only prove that it was all a fantasy.

Marta was eating lunch in her room, and I needed to get her attention. I could hear the hum of a radio through the kitchen wall.

"Marta?" I called, but she didn't answer.

I went to the door and tried the handle. It was locked, so I tapped on the doorframe. The radio went silent.

"Just a minute," she said, and listened for my exiting footsteps before she turned the radio back on.

I sat at the kitchen table waiting for Marta to resurface, but by the time she did I'd forgotten what I originally wanted to ask her.

"What is it?" she said.

"We're going to the Provost's for dinner," I announced.

"Good."

She turned to wash her plate.

I asked if she had ever met Melinda. She said she hadn't, but she knew one of her maids, Ana.

"What does Ana say about her?"

She finished drying the plate with a towel before she responded.

"Nothing bad."

"I can't imagine that's true. Come on, tell me. What does she say?"

She tried to brush it off, but I pressed her. "I won't tell anyone."

"Ana has to wear a uniform," she said. "Senhora likes fresh pastries in the house so that it smells sweet, but she doesn't eat them."

"I like fresh pastries," I said and winked at her, but Marta didn't think it was funny. She gave me a firm look and continued with the dishes.

"We're going to their home for dinner tomorrow night."

"Good. You'll see Ana." She put a shrimp salad in front of me and retreated to her room.

Then an unusual thing happened: the telephone rang. I picked it up, expecting that I would have to call Marta to translate. It was Celia. I could tell from the first breath—she paused before she said hello—and I nearly choked.

"Hello?"

"Hello. Linda?"

"Yes, hi." I swung the telephone cord around my neck. "You remember me."

"Of course I remember you. The woman with the shower cap."

I felt my face go warm. "Yes. That's me."

"Do you want to meet tomorrow?" she said.

"Yes."

"Good. I have a special place. Let's meet on the corner of Paulista and Augusta at three. I can't talk much now. I have to feed my dog."

I pressed the receiver close to my mouth.

"Sure," I said as the phone clicked off. I noticed Marta had put the Provost's figs in a granite bowl on the kitchen table. They were sticky ripe—I could smell them from across the room—and fruit flies had begun to swarm around the bowl. I pulled the trash can over and dumped them inside.

Chapter Twelve

For the first time in a long time I had a special friend and a special event. I was nervous—I checked the clock obsessively, calculating and recalculating time in my head. It was one, I was meeting Celia at three, and you'd be home at six, so I needed to be home by five thirty. Marta, briskly dragging a broom across the living room carpet, asked me where I was going.

"Where are you going?" she said, as calmly as that. I was wearing a silk dress and a barrette in my hair.

"To see a friend."

"Will you be home to eat?"

"I don't know."

"I'll leave dinner in the refrigerator."

I should have remembered then that we didn't need dinner. We were going to eat dinner at the Provost's apartment. But it didn't faze me—I kept fussing, throwing shoes on and off, twisting my hair into a knot and then letting it fall onto my shoulders, until it was quarter past two and I decided to go.

Better to be early than late, I thought, a novel thought for me, and left while Marta was in another room.

There is something intoxicating about a secret, like drinking too much dessert wine. As I walked to meet Celia, I passed by a coterie of old women with kerchiefs tied around their heads, pushing grocery carts up the sidewalk. I passed a line of young police officers wearing hats flopped to the side like French berets and AK-47s strapped across their chests. I passed an old tree that had nicks and bruises knotted into its trunk and branches intertwining with a telephone wire. I passed by a world that hovered around me, until Avenida Paulista opened up and I saw Celia.

I didn't realize that it was her at first. She wore a floor-length sarong that defined a graceful body that was before obscured, and she had a dog with her. As I approached, she was unraveling herself from the dog's leash while it barked at a motorcycle revving past.

"Celia?" I said from behind. She turned and I was struck by her watercolor face, soft and emotive. She stretched onto her tiptoes when she saw me, like she needed to reach up and out to greet me, and tugged the dog in closer to her.

"Linda. I hardly recognized you without your shower cap."

I touched my hair. "I only need it when it rains."

There was a vibration in the way our eyes connected, like we saw in each other something deep inside ourselves. I imagined that, in a parallel dimension, we were already holding hands, hugging each other in a long embrace, but in this reality we stood next to each other with excited hesitation, as strangers meeting only for the second time.

She leaned in to give me a kiss on the cheek and the dog jumped onto my legs with both paws.

"Claudius!" She pulled him down. "I'm sorry. He's very eager."

I ran my fingers through his thick and prickly fur.

"What kind of dog is he?"

"I don't know exactly. I found him years ago on the street." She pulled a biscuit out of her purse and fed it to him. "Shall we walk?"

I followed a couple steps behind as Claudius pulled Celia down the sidewalk. The dog required nearly unbroken vigilance. When he wasn't charging forward, he would stop abruptly to bark at a passing car, or to sniff a garbage pail, or to scratch his collar. A pink, unneutered sack swung between his hind legs as he trotted alongside Celia. If people tried to pet him, he'd clobber them with so much energy that they would have to back away. Celia apologized to them while Claudius was already on to the next, a string of saliva attached to his lower jowl.

"So," I said, hastening up to her so we could walk next to each other. "Where are we going?"

Celia smiled. "You don't like not knowing, do you?"

"I prefer to know, it's true."

"We're going to a play. And I'm not saying anything more." She pretended to zip up her lips.

"Oh," I said, feeling the disappointment nudge at me. I had envisioned us alone, side by side, talking away the hours. But, of course, I didn't want my disappointment to disappoint her. "What's the name of the play?"

"Uh-uh—I won't say anything more. It's part of the experience."

"Is it a well-known play?"

This made her laugh.

"I won't tell you!" Claudius squatted, back curled, in the middle of the sidewalk, and a hot stench sank into my nose. Celia took out a green plastic bag and tenderly picked up the waste. "I think you'll enjoy it. And some friends of mine will be there too."

Already I was nervous. "Sounds great," I said. "Which friends?"

"Oh, the usual crowd. Simone will be there. You'll love Simone." She tied the plastic bag closed. Simone, Celia explained, was one of her closest friends and had been with their theater company for almost ten years.

"Is she an actress?"

"She is, but we hired her as a stagehand because that's the job I had at the time." Celia had just begun managing the company when Simone applied. "I didn't know how good an actress she was. One of the best."

Simone, who was still Simão at the time, had walked into Celia's theater without a résumé or a head shot and told the teller at the ticket booth that she was looking for work. Both her parents and her boyfriend had disowned her after she decided to transition—she didn't have a place to live or any money. Celia hired her and let her live in the costume room in the attic until she collected enough paychecks to rent an apartment near Luz Station. Sometimes she and Celia would bring wine and sushi up the wooden ladder and eat and drink in taffeta skirts and pirate hats.

Celia tried to convince Simone to audition for a part, but when the next production came around, Simone refused. She had only ever acted in male roles, she told Celia. What if she wasn't any good? Auditions came and went. Celia pressed and pressed, but Simone evaded her. To earn more money, she began to pick up catering jobs, passing hors d'oeuvres around at cocktail parties.

I felt I understood Simone's fear. When you've been deprived of your natural self for so long, and then that self appears, the anxiety that you may stumble—out of pure, clumsy inexperience—can be overwhelming.

Celia turned in to an alley between a nightclub and a women's department store where mannequins and empty beer bottles had been discarded. She opened a wrought-iron door on the side of the building. The inside revealed a courtyard shaped like a small coliseum, circular and sunken in the middle, filled with people. Two children were running around, weaving through legs, and as soon as we walked in Claudius ran after them into the center of the crowd. We followed.

Celia introduced me to a man with a long gray beard and a peacock feather in his hat. He was talking to a woman with braids down to her knees, each one festooned with beads and gold clasps. Neither spoke English. Celia was my translator, a job she accepted enthusiastically. She paused to explain who someone was (Thiago, the drummer; Igor, the director; Elena, the actress). She would speak rapidly with them, laughing and gesturing wildly, and then she would pause to explain everything to me.

This process eventually became exhausting. I watched the conversations unfold in front of me, while Celia would pass me polite glances like salt at the dinner table. Claudius had curled up on the floor next to Celia's feet, eyes closed, and I wished I could do the same, that I had such an easy excuse to fall away.

The children ran by. One used my body as a hiding spot, while the other searched behind other adult legs.

"The children think that I am an inanimate object," I said into the corner of Celia's ear.

"Let's get a drink." She waved down a server, who brought us two caipirinhas with pineapples splayed on the plastic rims. "The performance is going to start soon."

The lights dimmed and the crowd began to assemble at small tables surrounding the stage. I followed Celia and Claudius to a table close to the front.

A drum troupe, three of them, emerged and set up in the back. One began to beat. Thud, thud, thud, thud. I could feel the vibration echo in the center of my chest. Some of the guests came around and handed us blindfolds. The man with the peacock feather tied a scarf around my face so that I no longer had a perception of how far away my face was from my hands or where Celia was sitting. I felt a gritty, wet surface brush against my hand. It was Claudius. He put his head on top of my leg, and I held on to him as an anchor.

When they announced that we could take off our blindfolds, two boxers stood in the center of the sunken space, wearing only red silk trunks and rubber guards in their mouths, their hands bare-knuckled and taped. I rubbed the bandages wrapped around my own palms. Each boxer had a stone in his hand. They crouched low, and one boxer picked up his right leg and swung it up and over the other boxer. Once his feet touched the ground, the other did the same, over and around, again and again, until it turned into a rhythmic motion, circles folding into circles. The drums followed. Badum, badum, badum, faster and faster.

Now the crowd really became excited. Everyone, Celia included, started to whistle and jeer and whip their blindfolds above their heads. The fighters were ignited by the audience's energy—the more we cheered, the closer they moved to each other, and the closer they moved, the more we cheered. Their slippery bodies were inches from each other, legs and arms twisting and crossing, the drums breaking through our roar like a summer storm, until one boxer landed the first blow. It was the fist with the stone. Crack. Right across the jaw. I froze and instinctively clutched my own face, as if I could taste the metal and grated skin inside my cheek. I looked at Celia, expecting equal shock, but she and the rest of the crowd had erupted in applause.

The two children were sitting on the floor, cross-legged, sharing a bowl of chocolate gelato. Once one boxer made the first hit, all hope vanished, and they both started to beat each other, blood splashing across the floor until it was dotted red like a poppy field. I couldn't take it. I did the only thing I could think to do—I put the blindfold back on.

Once the cheering stopped, I lifted the scarf from my eyes. Blood was everywhere. They had hit each other so consistently that both men lay crooked on the ground, unmoving, their faces smeared with blood. My cheeks were wet, but I couldn't tell if it was from tears or sweat. I thought they were dead. Claudius rose from underneath Celia, lurched toward the stage, and nudged one of their feet with his snout. I tried to grab on to his leash, but then I saw him lick the blood. Celia didn't stop him, so he continued licking until he had cleaned up an entire patch on the stage.

I sat dumbstruck and silent. After the cheering died down, the boxers leapt up, hugged each other, and bowed. The audience stood and applauded.

Celia turned to me, still clapping, and saw my dismay. She was puzzled at first, and then realized my confusion.

"Oh, Linda," she said and stroked my hand. "Querida, it's not real!"

She dragged her finger across a drop of blood that had landed on her arm and put it against her tongue. "See," she said and licked the tip of her finger.

I tried a lick myself. It tasted like flour and licorice.

"I didn't know," I said. "I was sure they were dead."

She consoled me, embracing my hand in hers from across the table, until a group of people swarmed in, congratulating her on the performance. It was her theater company's production. I sat for a bit, weighing if I should join her conversation, then decided to go search for Claudius. He had cleaned up half the stage by the time I found him.

We didn't stay much longer. I told Celia I needed to be

home. It was almost seven. I assumed she would stay without me, but she took a last sip of her pineapple caipirinha and said she'd walk out too.

On our way to the exit we ran into Simone.

"Menina," Celia said and embraced her.

Celia introduced me. Simone ducked her nose into her shoulder and smiled.

"Oi," she said and gave me a perfunctory kiss on the cheek, her eyes attentive like a cat's whiskers.

"Oi," I said back.

Simone spoke in an almost whisper and Celia translated what she said back.

"She wants to know if you liked the play," Celia said to me, and they both stood motionless, awaiting my answer.

I nodded vehemently, and Simone's face rose with satisfaction.

Celia and I said our goodbyes and then stepped out into the night. The mannequin bodies formed a ghostly mirage down the path to the street. Claudius stopped at various light poles to mark his territory along the way.

"So, tell me. What did you really think?" said Celia. "And don't just say what you think I want to hear."

I searched for the right words. In truth, I'd found the play uncomfortable, at times unwatchable. I often didn't know where to put my eyes, where my hands should go, if it would be appropriate to leave for the bathroom.

Celia continued. "I noticed you put your blindfold back on."

"Yes, at one point I did," I said. "I'm sorry. It's not that I didn't like it."

"I know. It's not easy to watch." She stopped walking, and Claudius glanced back at her. "But that's not the intention, either. I want to know—what did it remind you of?"

I wanted to say the right thing. I wanted her to take me seri-ously. I clicked through interpretations in my mind, rifling through possibilities as through an overstuffed file cabinet. Was it a metaphor for war? No. Masculinity? Too obvious. Patriar-chy? Domestic violence? Environmental collapse?

And then I said, "When we first met, I told you that I had thought about leaving my husband. Before we came to São Paulo."

Celia nodded.

"Well, I'm starting to realize this is a tendency I have. To fantasize about things that aren't in my life. To long for some-thing different."

As I said this, Claudius bumped into the side of my leg and knocked me off my balance.

"Here," I said and reached out my hand. "Let me hold him."

Celia passed me the leash and grazed the bandages on my hands in a way that sent goosebumps up my arms.

"The uncomfortableness of the play reminded me of how painful that frame of mind can be. To live in a constant state of transcendence. There is no real way to escape our selves."

Celia placed her hand on my shoulder. "You shouldn't try to escape yourself, Linda. I love you. You are linda."

A smile cropped up from deep inside me. She said "linda" as Marta had, small-el "linda," and we walked for a bit in silence as I allowed the glimmering halo of "I love you" to sink in.

"The boxers moved elegantly," I continued. I wanted to say more, to give her more praise. I didn't want our time together to end. "It was a nice contrast to the violence."

"Did you recognize the dance? The capoeira?"

I shook my head.

Capoeira, Celia explained, is martial arts, dance, drums, per-formance, and acrobatics invented by enslaved African people in Brazil. It's a huge part of the culture; everyone loves capoeira. Tourists pay money to see capoeira performances on São Paulo's streets.

"But do we think about where it originated?" she said. "Do we see the violence that gave us so much of our culture? Capoeira. Carnaval. Even feijoada."

We stopped in front of the subway entrance, and Celia picked up Claudius with both arms.

"That's what I want to do with my theater. I want to lift the mask and show that Brazil still has a lot of healing to do."

"I can understand that," I said. "I have a lot of healing to do too."

Celia began to descend the subway stairs.

"Yes. But always remember: Your healing should not come at someone else's expense."

By the time I got to the apartment, the backs of my heels were torn with blisters. I was lost in thought when I entered the kitchen. You were standing in front of the sink with the faucet on.

"Hi," I said.

"I've been waiting for hours." That's when I noticed you were in a suit. You had your good dress shoes on.

"I went for a walk. I got lost," I said. I was scrambling, trying to think up something to say that would soften the blow. I had forgotten about your dinner.

"I told you this morning to meet me at the apartment."

My mind searched and searched. I had no memory of remembering, and no memory of forgetting. I just remembered that I had never really wanted to go.

"We had dinner. With Eduardo and Melinda. Remember?"

"I'm sorry, Dennis. I went out for a walk to get some air. I felt so sick in the apartment— I thought I could take a walk through the park. But then I turned down the wrong road and it was dark. I didn't know where I was."

"I told them you were sick. We'll reschedule."

"I know this was important to you." I joined you at the sink and tucked my arms underneath yours. I could feel that your body was restricted, hardly responsive to my touch. I held on longer until you softened and rested your chin on the top of my head.

"Lately it's impossible to know what you're thinking," you said and pressed closer to me. I felt your hand move down the edge of your zipper and rub up against my skin.

"No, Dennis. Not now."

You held me tighter.

"I was just so angry. Sometimes it helps."

"Let's go to bed," I said.

We unwrapped the bandages in the kitchen and you helped me put on a new, fresh layer. We left arm in arm, through the hallway, toward the bedroom. The light from our open door shone brighter as we approached. We walked, and with each step exhaustion glazed my body, froze me in a sarcophagus of cause and effect. A husband and a wife closed inside a box of light.

Chapter Thirteen

Celia called me a few days later and told me that she wanted to teach me Portuguese. I agreed, knowing full well that these lessons were only an excuse for us to talk more often. One phone call turned into two, then three, until she called four or five times a week, all under the pretext that she was my teacher and I was her pupil. I would pour a glass of orange juice and sit on the laundry room floor, phone in my lap, and listen amused as she grappled with which words she wanted me to learn, before we would dissolve into stories about each other's lives.

My excitement over this new relationship felt like it was alive inside me, growing, wanting to be fed and stroked and played with. I told myself that I couldn't tell you about Celia, for fear that my sharing it with you would cause the relationship to mature too quickly. You might ask me questions about her, questions I might not have the answers to. You might ask to meet her; you might want to form a relationship with her on your own. I wanted to get to know her on my own terms. I liked having Celia all to myself. The fact that she was for me, and only me, made each interaction with her purely effervescent.

Still, the urge to tell someone, anyone, about her clawed inside me, yearning for a chance to jump out, run around in the open. One morning I blurted it out.

"I think I have a friend," I said to Marta. She was changing the sheets on our bed, and I was sitting on a chair by the window.

Without missing a beat, she said, "Is that who you talk to on the phone?"

I paused. I hadn't realized she had heard me on the phone.

"Yes," I said. "She's teaching me Portuguese."

Marta rolled the fitted sheet into a ball and tossed it toward the door. She smiled. "I don't hear much Portuguese. Just a lot of giggling."

It was a special power of Marta's, to always know without precisely knowing.

"What can I say. Portuguese makes me laugh?"

"Where did you meet this friend? At the university?"

"No," I said. "She's not with the university. Dennis doesn't know her."

I said this more defensively than I'd intended and held my breath, waiting for Marta to respond. She shook a pillow out of its case and let it fall to the floor.

"Actually," I continued, "maybe you shouldn't mention her to Dennis. Not that you would, but—"

Marta stopped what she was doing and examined my face. Instinctively I began to chew on my thumbnail.

"It's none of my business," she said and walked out of the room with the laundry bundled in her arms.

After this conversation, I began to feel very exposed around Marta, like she had the ability to identify the worst parts of me, parts of me that I didn't even know existed. Celia embodied the balance of safety and adventure I had been longing for after my father died, but I also felt shameful for keeping her a secret from you. The only way I could do both—stay honest with you while hiding my relationship with Celia—was to deny the excitement I felt about her. I told myself that our relationship wasn't important enough to share, that it was an afterthought to my days, even though that was the exact opposite of true. I was constantly distracted by thoughts about Celia.

Marta made this denial difficult. She was the vigilant eye, always around, always aware. After Celia started to call more regularly, I would crouch into the corner of the laundry room with the phone receiver tight against my ear, trying to go unnoticed, even when Marta was just on the other side of the door. There was something so precious about our phone conversations, something so fragile and singular, how she'd unwrap each word like a present. It reminded me a bit of the time I went to visit my mother early on in our relationship, and you wrote me a note for every day I was gone. You even made a little box to store the notes in, each carefully folded into a tight square. One had a drawing of a heart with my name in the middle. Another a long rant about a text you were reading for your dissertation. It was an entrance into each other, and my conversations with Celia contained a similar tenderness.

"Lembra, that's a good one. Eu lembro, você lembra."

"Eu lembro," I repeated. "I remember."

Another day she taught me "I need." Preciso.

"Eu lembro. Eu preciso. I remember. I need."

I began to notice the shapes that my mouth preferred, the sounds that came easily and those that wouldn't.

"I know. Saudades," she said.

"I've heard this word before."

"It's like 'I miss you,' but it's much more than that."

It's closer. It's felt more deeply.

"You can have saudades for someone who's right next to you," she explained. "I can have saudades for you before you've gone."

Eventually, though, the Portuguese lessons stopped entirely, and we felt comfortable opening up to each other as soon as we picked up the phone. I would tell her about Hartford and Boston, my times of loneliness in Brazil, about us. I'd often jot notes as we were talking, and I'd return to them days later to reflect and recollect. Here's a selection of ones that I've kept over the years. I've compiled as much as eu lembro.

THE LABORER

I told her about my father, how he'd been a worker his entire life, committed to a string of union jobs, each lasting six or seven years, the serial monogamist of employment. When I was young he had a job setting up tents, those big white tents people order for weddings and graduations. I remember how magical it was as a child to run around the empty tent before they set up the tables and chairs, barefoot in the dewy grass, the sun echoing a dull light across the canvas peaks. I'd pretend he was a giant, hammering tree trunks into the ground, and he'd pretend I was a rabbit that he wanted to eat for dinner. I still remember the excited fear of running away, and the joy of being scooped up into his large arms and nuzzled.

Before the tent job he worked at a moving company, painted houses, bartended (though he quit that when he quit drinking), and worked as a hardware store clerk. When he worked at the tent job during the day, he took adult education classes at night to get his electrician's license. That was the last job he had before he got Alzheimer's. Everything my father did showed in his body—his callused hands and cracked cheekbones, the burns across his arms from live wires, the knobs he developed in his elbows from arthritis. When his body began to deteriorate—when he could no longer control his bladder and the angry confusion that followed, my father, the laborer, the man who would pick me up by the armpits and lift me over his head—it was like he lost his whole identity.

REAL ECUADORIANS

Celia's childhood was different from mine. Her parents were bohemians who inherited money from her grandparents, and she found this fact shameful from the time she learned what inheritance meant. She told me about the decision she made as a teenager to move to Ecuador, when she declared to her parents that she wanted to relinquish her possessions and sell jewelry in a stand on the side of the road. She was eighteen; they told her she could go, understanding well enough that she would return. She took several buses across the continent and checked in to a hostel close to the beach. She would sit on the shore alone, eating shrimp ceviche from a paper cup. The first three weeks she had the hostel room mostly to herself, except for one quiet Australian woman who stayed only for a few days. Then two men arrived on vacation for the weekend. They were from the center of Ecuador, but they had been coming to the coast all their lives. They offered to take Celia out to the bars. She agreed, thrilled that she would learn the local spots from two real Ecuadorians.

The next morning, she woke up next to an abandoned barge on the beach, with no memory of getting there. Her purse had been stolen. She cried outside a fish market until she decided she would call her mother, who wired her money immediately. She returned home, and a few months later, she enrolled in acting school in São Paulo.

CRANBERRY GRANOLA

Celia burned through romance, it was her gunpowder, and it made me realize even more how much you and I had built our lives on comfortable love, on an understanding of commitment and shared details. You knew which side of the bed I preferred, what size toothbrush I bought, my favorite kind of cranberry granola. You and I met through a mutual friend in Boston, when you were still in your PhD program. Celia wanted to know everything about Boston, but it was difficult to conjure the specific images and sounds that I had once known so well.

One memory that came vividly to mind was when we had our apartment in the South End and would take walks to the Pru, Copley Square, and through the Boston Common and Public Garden. I remembered once passing by the Berkeley Community Garden, when all the plants were brown and covered for the winter, and a woman in a green straw hat was planting bulbs. When we got to the Public Garden, you stopped and took out your camera, a brand-new Nikon F, and asked me to sit on one of the statues of the bronze ducks so that you could take a picture. It's such a small, underdeveloped memory. Nothing happened that day: we went to the Pru, looked at the stores, then turned around and went home. Celia loved it. She asked me to describe Boston again, and again, and again.

PATTI

After her experience in Ecuador, Celia gave up men for a long time. She had moved fluidly between men and women since she was a teenager; this was the first time she decisively said she only wanted one, and she chose women. She began dating one of her best friends, a woman named Patti, who baked glazed chocolate cakes and wore ruby cat-eye glasses. Celia described the relationship as romantic psychiatry, where Celia was the patient who couldn't be sorted out, always longing for more time to undo the complex knots in her mind, and in repayment Patti made love to Celia however Celia wanted to be made love to, which, Celia realized as she said it out loud, wasn't repayment at all, but one more way in which Patti would give and Celia would happily take.

MARRY A JEWISH WOMAN

Celia's grandparents were Jewish immigrants who came to Brazil from Poland to escape the Holocaust. They didn't know each other in Poland; they met in Santos. Two Poles adjusting to the tropics.

She described Santos as a rusted seaport with steamships rimming the horizon, cobblestone roads, and shrines devoted to Pelé. Her grandparents met working on an assembly line at a textile mill. After work, her grandfather would hang around the piers waiting for the cargo ships to arrive. He'd bring a pack of cigarettes and have a smoke with the traders.

"They wanted to know where to meet women," she said. "He told me he only gave them directions."

After years of working on the line, her grandfather was promoted to manager and saved enough money to propose to Celia's grandmother. They were bonded by their love of the Jewish faith and their knowledge of textiles. What they didn't learn in the factory, they researched at night before reading the Torah in bed.

Eventually Celia's grandfather formed a side business on the piers. He inspected rug shipments to check for imperfections and charged a fee to the traders. The business grew, and he began trading himself. By 1973 her grandparents had offices in Santos and São Paulo, employees, a teenage son named Ronaldo, and a rug-trading business that spanned the globe—India, the Philippines, Egypt.

"Their hope was that he would one day take over the business," Celia said of her father. "But it was the seventies. He didn't want to work in an office."

While his parents were in Santos tending to the business, Ronaldo stayed at their second home, in São Paulo, dropping LSD and building guitars. His parents gave him an allowance on top of food and a home. He had no urgency to leave his life.

"I wonder sometimes if it had to do with the Holocaust," Celia said, her voice low, as though she were asking herself.

"How do you mean?"

"They wanted him to be happy. They wanted him to feel freedom, deep, in a way that they couldn't."

"Did they remember the war? They were children when they came to Brazil."

She paused.

"Of course. Even I remember the war. It's in my bones."

The one rule they had for Ronaldo was that he had to marry a Jewish woman. Instead he fell in love with a girl from Lebanon, Celia's mother, at a bookstore café in Pinheiros. His parents never recovered. They continued to give him money, even after they both died, but they never recovered.

THE NIGHT BANDITS

Celia inherited her family's house in São Paulo—a two-story home with a roof covered in plants, at the bottom of a steep hill in Perdizes—when her grandparents passed. Celia required solitude, and the house gave her that, but she still suffered through deep bouts of loneliness. So she found a couple to move in with her, Karina and Rafael, whom she knew through friends of friends.

Karina and Rafael were lovers and graffiti artists. "The Night Bandits," they were called. Os Bandidos da Noite. They tagged the tops of skyscrapers with the silhouette of a female bandit, her face obscured with a black bandanna, her hair a single wisp trailing behind her. São Paulo had many talented graffiti artists, but it was the scale and height that gave the Night Bandits a particular edge.

Celia described Karina as a woman sculpted by clay drawn from a river: earthy, essential, hard in the sun, smooth when wet. A Capricorn sun sign, Celia explained, which meant she was grounded and persistent. Karina didn't care about anyone who wasn't born with dirt in their pockets and mud in their hair. She took her graffiti art with Rafael particularly seriously. She refused to reveal how they scaled such enormous buildings, sometimes forty stories high, at night, unseen, to spray-paint a twenty-foot-tall woman. Onlookers could see the image clearly from the street, her body so dark it looked like she had crashed through the building. She wouldn't even tell Celia after living in her house for more than five years.

Rafael was a drifter, a talker, a charmer. Celia's house was the first place he'd called home for more than a year, a fact that Celia took particular pride in, as though she was able to give him something that no other person had, perhaps not even Karina. Rafael often went to Celia when he and Karina fought. One night, Celia took him to the emergency room because Karina threw a small flowerpot at his head, cracking open his eyebrow. When Celia arrived at home and walked into the scene, Karina was still yelling at Rafael even after she had thrown the pot, while Rafael soaked up a dishrag with blood and potting soil. Karina insisted Rafael had provoked her, that she loved him but that he was killing her, then she stormed into their bedroom and locked the door. Celia convinced Rafael to go with her to the hospital.

Rafael got eleven stitches. To distract him while the doctor threaded through his skin, Celia tried to remind Rafael of why he loved Karina: you scale buildings together, you inspire art in each other, you paint each other's bodies, you bring her coffee in bed, you listen to records and sing jazz and play guitar.

"You want to know how?" he said to Celia and told the doctor that he had permission to tell the entire hospital the secret process behind the Night Bandits. He didn't care. "We break into a building in the morning, usually through the freight elevator, and hide on the roof for an entire day. It's miserable— I spend the day in a panic. Then after eating nuts and dried papaya and drinking coffee from a thermos, when it's too dark for pedestrians to see, I lower Karina in a metal crate with chains strapped to a pulley. I worry about her falling, about the chains giving out. Sometimes I wake in the middle of the night with that sound in my head, the clack clack clack of loose chains rattling against the building." He touched his palm to his wound and winced.

"Maybe I should just let go! Maybe we'd both be better off!" he said, and the doctor gave him a pad of gauze to dab his tears.

By the time Celia and Rafael returned home from the hospital, Karina had unlocked herself from the bedroom and moved to the living room. She was splayed across the couch, naked, her body painted with his favorite color—citron yellow—which he found so amazing that he forgot he was angry. But then he remembered and cried to her, "You can't throw our plants at me, Karina!" His anger softened when she pressed her yellow body against his and whispered, "Eu sei, eu sei, querido." Celia listened to them make love on the other side of the wall while she swept up the shattered clay.

Chapter Fourteen

We left in a hurry for our rain check dinner at the Provost's. I didn't even have time to dress myself properly. You roamed the apartment, picking bits of lint from the bedroom carpet, straightening books on the coffee table, checking your tie in the bathroom mirror. Circling, circling, and in my heart I felt stunted, like my arms couldn't reach out far enough to break your frenzied rhythm. I took out the iron and pressed a white cotton dress, dashed on a smear of pink lipstick. This was the first time I could leave the apartment without bandages—my palms had finally healed enough. On our way out the door you mentioned, ever so slightly, that we had left on time for once. I asked you to grab the bouquet of tiger lilies and walked out the door first.

The Provost sent us a driver, a man with a dark, glassy face that reflected like a puddle in the sun. He drove us to the neighborhood of Morumbi, where the Provost and his wife lived in a high-rise building with a revolving gold door. The driver found a spot just outside the building and told us he'd wait for us there until we were done. You thanked him and asked me if

I thought we should tip him. I said I didn't know, and so we decided that we would tip him on the way home. We approached the doormen and told them we were there to see Dr. and Mrs. Miranda.

"I work with the doctor," you said.

The Provost had forgotten to give the front desk our names, so they asked for identification. I had left my wallet at home—desculpa, desculpa, I apologized. One of the doormen held on to your card while he rang the Provost's apartment. The other inspected us with a tight mouth. In an attempt at humor, I can only assume, you passed a five note across the marble counter. The doorman looked at the money and then back down at his computer screen. You returned it to your jacket pocket. One of the Provost's maids picked up the phone and said to let us up.

In the elevator you laughed.

"The security in this building is stricter than the White House."

We went up to the thirty-first floor and were let out into a wide and tall marbled hallway.

"Apartment D," you said. "He said to listen for the barking dogs."

As promised, we heard dogs yapping behind a gold-plated door, and after one knock the Provost's wife appeared with two white balls of fur bouncing at her side. Our eyes met, then she looked down at my shoes and back up at you. I pressed my already wrinkled skirt against my legs and watched you absorb the luxury of her appearance, her large emerald earrings and black wrap dress, how effortless it seemed for her to host us.

"Dennis," she said and greeted you with a kiss. "Oi, Linda." She turned to me and pressed her cheek to mine. "Come, come in. Let me get you something to drink."

I handed her the bouquet of lilies, and she smelled them

deeply, then passed them to a maid, who put them in a vase and brought them upstairs. When I thought of the Provost's apartment, I had envisioned an old wooden home filled with books and antique tables, but it was the opposite. Their taste was quite modern. The apartment sparkled like sugar: white curtains draped in a slinky cursive, Lucite chairs and marbled surfaces, several jade Buddhas smiling from side tables. Melinda grabbed the dogs with both arms and handed them to another maid, who locked them in a room upstairs. She took us through the sitting room and into the dining area, where Eduardo sat with an aperitif in a short crystal glass, flipping through a world atlas.

"Dennis!" He stood to shake your hand. "You must see this book that Alfonzo gave me. You know Alfonzo, don't you? The economist?"

He gave me a long hug and then ushered you to the table. You both leaned over the book, palms pressed against the table like two conquistadors. Just as I was about to come see what you were studying, Melinda appeared by my side.

"There you are," she said, and I saw the conversational bars clank down around me.

We all milled in the dining room for appetizers, a cheese plate and ham, fresh papaya and croquettes. The Provost made a few jokes about his wife's shopping habits, and we all laughed. He teased her about her remedial knowledge of soccer, and we laughed again. She dipped the end of her finger in her glass of rum and daintily tasted it, for no other reason, it seemed, than the amusement of sucking on her finger. When it was almost time for dinner, we all sat at one end of the long table, the two couples facing each other. I looked to you for a spot of acknowledgment, but your entire being was turned toward the Provost, engaged in some conversation about university politics.

The Provost's wife lit a cigarette and offered one to me. I declined. My ability to engage had shrunk low, crouched somewhere next to my tailbone. The conversation had wandered meaninglessly for too long—I was finding it more and more difficult to pay attention. I thought what would happen if I shook things up a bit. How they would react if I bit your arm? Or lit a fire in the kitchen. I was grateful when the two maids brought dinner out to the table: a bowl of pão de queijo, dishes of yucca flour, picanha, and moqueca de camarão, a stew made with coconut milk and shrimp.

"Because you don't eat beef," said the Provost's wife, smiling at me. "And chicken is too boring."

I thanked her, and as I did, one of the women presented a tray of picanha in front of you and the Provost, the centers pink and puddling in fatty juice. I could practically feel the saliva pool underneath your tongue.

"I'll eat the camarão with you," Melinda said and pulled a piece of shrimp off her fork with her teeth.

"Everything looks delicious," you announced.

"Ana did it all." Melinda gestured to the kitchen, where a young girl wearing a tan uniform stood.

The Provost clinked his fork against the glass.

"Gente!" he said, sitting upright, then covered his mouth, as if to stop a burp. "Desculpa, Linda. In English. Thank you both for coming. I hope you like the food that my wife very carefully prepared." He winked at her. "Eat, drink, we're all friends here."

He was drunk already. The bottle of rum tilted into your glass, led by your boss's heavy hand, and I saw your cheeks flower, your teeth blossom. The Provost's wife lit another cigarette, her plate of food untouched.

"Melinda," you started, cutting a piece of steak. "Have you been to the United States?"

"Yes, many times," she said. "We were just in Miami for a conference."

"And what did you think?"

"Miami is beautiful. I love the ocean there, and the little plants that grow on the sidewalk." She released the smoke slowly from the corner of her mouth. "But the airport was horrible. They made me take my shoes off at security, grabbed on to my body, checked all of my bags. It was horrible."

"I agree. It's a bit extreme," you said. "But what else can we do? In this day and age."

I had always known you as politically left, but the terrorist attacks in New York had morphed your opinion of the world. You knew someone who died in the towers. Our nation's safety was suddenly a priority to you. You apologized to Melinda for her experience at the airport and continued to eat your food.

"Look," the Provost said and gripped your shoulder hard, shaking it a bit. "The United States is a beautiful country, but it has many problems. Here in Brazil, we elected a president who was a factory worker, who came from nothing, and now he's president of the country. Is that not what you call the American dream?"

Ana stood next to the table, pouring more water. The Provost's wife took a puff of her cigarette and waved her hand, as if to dismiss her to the kitchen.

Eduardo explained that he'd met Lula when he came to speak at USP during his campaign, and according to Eduardo (though Melinda refuted this) he and Lula had kept in touch here and there since he took the presidency. Though you and I knew Lula for his championing of the poor, Eduardo seemed to admire Lula for his global impact. As he saw it, Lula had done what the brutal military dictatorships before him could not: he'd made Brazil an economic leader.

"I predict," he said, holding up his glass, "that by 2010, Brazil will be the superpower of the world." He chuckled and looked directly at you. "The United States should worry! You have George Bush!"

The comment settled like dust on the conversation. A sense of pride was triggered in you, shown only in a slight tilt of your head.

You leaned back in your chair, smiling, and said, "We'll see."

The Provost's wife dropped her cigarette into her water glass, then called for Ana, who brought a porcelain ashtray with a picture of Marilyn Monroe in the center. Melinda put a cigarette to her mouth, and Ana struck a match for her.

"Obrigada, Ana." Once Ana had left, Melinda said to me, quietly, "I love her. She is like family."

A physical discomfort had begun to grow inside me. It started from below and spread up, a warmth that felt like it was slowly expanding. At first I thought it was the wine washing over me. And then I thought maybe I had been sitting for too long, that I needed to move around. But the more it crept underneath, the more I realized that it wasn't just the conversation.

"Sorry," I said. "I need to use the restroom. Where is it?"

Melinda called for Ana to show me to the bathroom. We walked through the living room where we had entered, past their library, and into another hallway, where she brought me to a powder room between two closed doors.

"Aqui," said Ana.

"Obrigada."

I closed the door and pulled my underwear down to my knees. A fragrance, like baby powder, wafted from my underwear and in my urine. Was it the food? Had the air in the house infiltrated my bladder? I wiped myself with some toilet paper and noticed a diluted red stain on the tissue. "Fuck," I said out loud. "Fuck." I checked my underwear again and saw the brown-red stain that had seeped through and dotted the back of my dress. Panicked, I checked underneath the sink for tampons, but I only found candles and cleaning products, so I wrapped a thick pad of toilet paper around my underwear.

I opened my palms and traced the dark, purple lines where scars had begun to form. I wanted to cry. Between my legs, a drop of blood fell into the toilet water, tumbled and expanded, like a time-lapse flower opening for the sun. The realization burst, a tiny sparkle of a thought, that no matter how steadily I trained my mind, my body reigned over all.

Could it be that I was somehow more animal than you? Animals pee where they want, shit where they want, bleed where they want. It's true that I had imagined biting your arm in the middle of dinner. Not hard—just enough to rattle your attention. And here I was, dabbing my bloodied underwear, the tears just an itch in my nose but soon to fall to my cheeks. Delicate—is that what you need from your animal wife? She who lives inside a body she cannot control.

I inspected my face in the mirror and begged for an answer, begged my body to contain itself for only another hour. I thought maybe I could just sit on the toilet until all the blood drained out of me. But if I stayed in the bathroom too long, you would come to check on me. I imagined you opening the bathroom door and a wave of blood crashing over you. Or I could leave now, tell them I'd fallen ill and needed to go home. How many times could I cry sick before they started to wonder?

I opened the door and poked my head out. Ana stood in the library dusting the books next to a radio.

"Ana," I whispered. "Ana."

She turned and dropped the duster on the floor.

"Tampon," I said to her. "Tampon. Por favor."

Her eyes told me that she did not understand, so I pointed in between my legs.

"Blood. I have blood. Tampon."

She didn't say anything—she stared at me, studied my face, and then went into the closed room next door. I clenched every muscle in my body and prayed that she'd understood me. Just a few seconds later she returned and revealed a small cotton capsule in her hand.

"Thank you," I said. "Thank you so much."

I thought about hugging her, and she smiled back, but it was the kind of smile one might offer a sobbing stranger on the street. Pity. She went back to dusting, and I hid back inside the bathroom. The tampon unwrapped from the plastic like an insect out of its shell. I inserted it with my finger and washed my hands, a thin twirl of blood disappearing into the drain. Instantly my body felt plugged, controlled.

When I returned to the dining room, the conversation had turned to Marta.

"We do like her very much," you said, scraping the last bit of rice and beans from your plate. "She's professional. It's helpful that she knows English. Her cooking is delicious. But there was one incident that was a bit . . . concerning."

As I made my way to my seat, you followed me with your eyes. By a miracle, the chair was as white as when I'd arrived.

"Linda, we're talking about Marta. Tell them about the suit."

I felt the color sink from my face. The bottoms of my feet tingled with hesitation, like I'd approached an open airplane door.

"Do we have to talk about this? It's nothing."

The Provost chimed in. "Well, now you've piqued my interest."

"I came home one day and my linen suit was in the laundry room, soaking wet, with a huge blue ink stain on it."

"Huge might be an exaggeration, Dennis." I pinched your thigh underneath the table. You looked at me but brushed it off.

"The strange thing is, I'd just had that suit cleaned. I wore it on my first day teaching."

The Provost's wife stamped out her cigarette in the Monroe ashtray and poured some more wine.

"Be careful. She might be stealing from you. I had a maid steal a pair of diamond earrings—"

"Querida," the Provost interrupted. "Those earrings fell down the kitchen drain. We found them." He spoke with a tired breath, as if this was a conversation they'd had many times before.

"Nonsense. She threw them down there when she suspected I knew!"

The three of you talked in triangles, bouncing from point to point with measured intention. You had transformed before my eyes—I hardly recognized you. You draped your arm across the back of my chair with a blasé self-importance. You talked as if words came in valueless abundance, as if you had plenty to spend. I became self-conscious about how quickly I was blinking and the pace of my breath. These automatic actions had somehow turned manual. Surely, I was blinking too much, breathing unevenly.

"Dennis, it's just a suit." This was the wrong thing to say. You looked at me, and I tried to apologize with my eyes.

The Provost's wife brought her elbows to the edge of the table and leaned forward. "I say confront her. Threaten to fire her if she doesn't confess."

"Meu Deus," said the Provost. "Maybe we should change the subject. My wife's had too much to drink, I think."

She rolled her eyes and leaned toward you even farther, her

breasts pressed over the table. "He makes jokes when he knows I am right."

When it seemed like there would be no escape from this conversation, that we were trapped here for the rest of the night, the doorbell rang.

"Who is it?" said the Provost to his wife. "I didn't hear the front desk call."

"I don't know, my darling. Perhaps you should go see?" She lit another cigarette.

The Provost grunted as he stood, like his body had stiffened from sitting too long, and hobbled into the living room. We all sat quietly and listened to the door open, the murmur of two deep voices, and the return of his heavy footsteps.

"Dennis, it's the driver. His wife just went into labor. He wants to know if you could leave now so he can go to the hospital."

At first you looked inconvenienced and I thought you might say no. But instead you said, "Yes, yes, of course. Linda, are you ready?"

More than ever, I wanted to say, and nodded. "Maybe we should take a taxi?"

"I'm sure it's fine," said the Provost. "Childbirth tends to take a while."

We left our plates dirty on the table without even a small taste of the brigadeiros that Ana had made. On the way out you asked the driver if he'd rather we call a taxi, but he seemed too panicked to change his mind, so we got into the car and drove silently, with just the occasional deep sigh from the front seat. The car stopped in front of our building, and you reached for my hand.

"That was a nice dinner," you said.

We exited on opposite sides of the car. As the driver sped off,

I realized that we never tipped him, but I didn't have the energy to mention it to you.

You waved to him from the street. "Good luck with your wife!"

When we got back into the apartment, you poured us two glasses of mango juice and we sat at our small kitchen table, on two wooden chairs, just for a few minutes until we retired to the bedroom. You fell asleep as soon as your body reached the bed.

I lay awake for hours. The question spun through my thoughts: Why didn't I confess? I was the one who had ruined the damn suit. And now what? Would you take your suspicions out on Marta? The whole conversation seemed like a performance for the Provost's wife, a spinning coin that began to wobble, so you fought desperately to keep it in motion. I had to believe you didn't actually think Marta was at fault. I had to believe it, or else I'd have to believe I was a reckless person, and in that moment, I couldn't bear the thought.

Chapter Fifteen

When I woke the next morning, a pink cloud of a stain had dried underneath me. Marta offered to wash it. I cried in front of her while holding the stained sheet in my hand.

"Why are you crying?" she asked.

I was hormonal and guilty. I told her I missed home. That I missed something familiar.

"What's something familiar?"

A peanut butter and jelly sandwich was the best solution I could find. I tried to explain to Marta what peanut butter was, but she didn't understand what I meant, so she asked me to come help her find it. We walked to a store that looked, from the outside, like a car garage, with a big sliding door that opened vertically to the street. I followed Marta around the aisles as she collected our everyday food—sliced cheese and ham for break-fast, jelly and Catupiry, papaya, mango, onions, brown beans, and bread—but I couldn't find the peanut butter. She suggested we try another store a few blocks up. It was midday so the streets were filled with people out for lunch, restaurants with tables open onto the streets, men in blazers and women in sharp blouses, sipping iced beers in the sun.

Marta's knees were bothering her; though she never admitted it to me, I could tell by the way she would straighten one leg as we climbed the uphill sidewalk. I began to tell her about something, what it was I can't remember, and she kept having to turn her head to hear me.

"Sim," she'd respond, glancing between me and the sidewalk ahead.

I told her that I could help carry the groceries, but she insisted I only take the small items, a loaf of bread and an egg carton, while she had three plastic bags hanging from each arm. I think that she felt sorry for me. She wore rubber Havaianas, blue ones, with a Brazilian flag on the strap. Right as she turned to ask me again what it was I had said, one of the sandals wedged into a hole in the sidewalk, a misplaced brick where they were doing construction. Her knee gave out. I heard the fall before I saw it—the quick rustle, pat-crack against the ground, Marta's deep bellow. A jar of strawberry jam, to go with the peanut butter, rolled into the road.

I dropped the eggs and rushed to her. "Marta." I reached my hand out. "Are you okay?"

She didn't respond, still hunched on the ground, her hands braced against the cement. Four or five people who were sitting outside a restaurant saw what had happened and hurried to her rescue. I stood frozen, unsure how or where to enter, and watched as they took each of her arms, one picked up the groceries, another talked to her soothingly. She stood and hugged the man who'd lifted her up, then hugged the woman who had consoled her, and then held the hand of the woman who'd retrieved the groceries. I stood, watching, the loaf of bread squashed by my feet.

"Marta. Are you okay?" I asked again, but still she didn't respond.

"Obrigada, gente," she said to them, dusting off her dress, and slipped her sandals back on.

Then she walked off. She picked up the grocery bags and crossed the street, away from me, toward the apartment. The people returned to their lunch, one watching me watch her as he ate a sliver of white fish.

Through the branches of a walnut tree, a breeze shook the leaves loose until they drifted down to the ground. Marta was already far gone, but still I called out to her, wanting her to turn around:

"Marta! Let me help you!"

She kept walking, as if dizzy, the hem of her dress swinging with each step. Later she would explain that she had been rattled—that the fall had made her forget why she left the apartment in the first place, so she instinctively went back. I would always remember that exact feeling, the feeling that I hadn't been the one to help her, that a group of strangers had before I did, and that I was a fleeting asteroid in the grand scheme of her universe.

I picked up the broken eggs and followed. I tried to hurry to her, but she made a traffic light that I didn't, and after that there was no catching up. I stayed light-years behind, still watching her, a dribble of yolk trailing me all the way home.

Chapter Sixteen

I felt closed in, claustrophobic, after dinner at the Provost's. I longed to see Celia. My hand moved comfortably to the telephone, dialed Celia's number, placed the receiver delicately against my ear. It was a Friday morning. She picked up with a just-woken hello.

"Alô?"

"Celia?"

"Falando."

"It's Linda. Did I wake you?"

She paused.

"Linda. Are you all right?"

Maybe she sensed the tremor in my voice—the nerves rose to my throat.

"Could I see you today? I'm fine. Just a little down."

"Yes, sure." I heard her ask something of someone else in the room. "You can come here to my house if you want."

She gave me directions by bus, but said it would take over an hour, so I decided to get a taxi at the stand outside the park. The driver wore a brown suit and the car smelled like rose water. We drove up Brigadeiro and crossed over Paulista, through the financial malaise of gray and brown skyscrapers, and into the orchid-lined streets of Jardins and Pinheiros. I hadn't ventured this far north before. The buildings in Pinheiros were covered in colorful graffiti—each side street revealed another geometric mural. I saw garbage bins filled with green coconuts, each with a straw sticking from the top, and cafés brimming onto the sidewalks.

Celia lived at the end of a short brick path in Perdizes, a hidden right turn at the bottom of a hill. She called it "the village." The taxi left me at the end of her street, and I walked up the path, passing by stray cats sprawled across the sun-warmed bricks, to her house on the far side of the dead end. She'd instructed me to knock on the front window when I arrived. I did. No one answered. I tried again, rapping harder. I had the thought that I should turn around, that maybe I'd gotten the wrong house, when Celia pulled back the curtain and pointed me toward the front door. She stood with her arms ready for an embrace and her hair slicked back from a shower.

"Sorry!" she said and kissed me on both cheeks. "We're on the roof."

She led me up two flights of stairs, the first to her bedroom and an office, the second through the office and up a set of winding mosaic steps to a weathered and expansive rooftop. The ground was still wet from the plants she had watered: large, pink-petaled flowers with orange stalks jutting from the center. She had hanging vines, cactuses, a row of banana leaf trees and palms. There were two couches that had been left in the rain, the fabric marked with dried water stains, and beanbag chairs that had been left in the sun, the red plastic faded to peach. On one of the beanbags were her roommates, Rafael and Karina. Os Bandidos da Noite. Karina was underneath Rafael with her legs curled around him.

Rafael heard us come up and lifted himself off of Karina to greet us.

"Bom dia, Linda. Como vai sua tia?" He laughed and, seeing I hadn't, clarified: "It's a joke."

"I'm going to finish making lunch," Celia said and gave me a squeeze on the elbow. "Stay with Karina and Rafael for a bit?"

Rafael led me to the couch in the shade, but Karina stayed put. I sensed immediately that she didn't appreciate my arrival. She liked it even less that Rafael left her to come sit with me. She straightened her back like a swan shaking its hind feathers and waved her arm in the air.

"Oi," she said and picked up a beauty magazine from the cement floor.

Instantly, Rafael began asking me questions: What did I think of Brazil? What did I think of São Paulo? What was the biggest difference between Brazil and the U.S.? Which did I like better?

I think Brazil is very beautiful, I told him, from what I've seen in pictures. São Paulo is not one thing, but I know it is sprawling. The biggest difference is the language, it is the heat, it is the way people laugh, the way they eat lunch, how the children play soccer, the showerheads, the lack of ice cubes.

"I haven't decided which I like better," I said and poured a glass of water from a pitcher on the foldout table.

Rafael explained that he had had an affinity for the United States since he was a child. His body was covered in American tattoos: Samuel L. Jackson in *Pulp Fiction* on his forearm, an anchor on his shoulder with the quote "Not all who wander are lost" in cursive, an outline of the state of Texas on his foot.

"My grandfather took me there when I was six," he said, running his finger over the lines on his foot bones.

"That's a serious devotion," I said. "Getting another country's state tattooed."

He seemed embarrassed for a moment, like he hadn't realized how obvious it was until he met an actual American. But then a smile spread across his freckled, broth-colored face, his grizzled hair only adding to his attractiveness.

"Most of all, I am Brazilian," he said in perfect English and puffed out his chest to reveal a Brazilian flag on his breastbone.

He told me about how he would fantasize about America when he'd sit on his mother's bed and watch the movie *Dirty Dancing*. She would yell at him for loosening her perfectly tucked linens as he ran around the mattress pretending he was Patrick Swayze. He wanted to go to a camp with wooden lodges and pine trees and stacks of pancakes with perfect squares of butter on top. He imagined that in the U.S. democracy prevailed, not like the corrupt politicians in Brazil who embezzled government money, or the police officers who shot innocent people on the street.

"Does everyone eat peas?" he asked, pretending to shovel spoonfuls in his mouth.

"Maybe some families."

"How about hot dogs?"

I smirked. It was hard not to be amused by his line of questioning.

"Sure, everyone eats hot dogs."

I could see Karina, not so far away, slumped over in the beanbag chair, a creeping fern circling her feet. Her hair cascaded over her shoulders and around the taut plastic sides. She had opened her blouse to let the sun in and occasionally fanned her neck with a beauty magazine. It appeared she was enthralled by the articles she flipped through, licking her finger every time she turned a page so that it made a loud snapping noise. But I could tell that she wasn't actually engaged. She was beautiful, but not interested in beauty. The magazine served as a decoy so that Rafael wouldn't realize she was listening to his every word.

"I see you love the United States," I said, nodding toward Karina. "What about her?"

"Who?"

"Karina."

"Karina? She's the love of my life."

"That's sweet."

"I would marry her if she believed in it."

He shouted "Karina!" as though she was on the roof of the adjacent building. He motioned for her to sit near him. "Vem aqui!"

She stared at him with crackling eyes, then turned away from us, her back creased and damp.

"Celia tells me you are graffiti artists," I said.

"Karina is the real artist. I am her assistant."

He said this with forced modesty.

"Karina is a visionary. She has dreams about the images she paints and wakes me in the night to go find a building." He looked at her back as he said this. "Karina doesn't . . . how do you say? Karina doesn't have a clock." He searched for the words. "No. Karina doesn't have time?"

The fact that Rafael kept repeating her name over and over in a language that she didn't understand wasn't lost on Karina's ears. By the fourth or fifth or sixth mention, she was fed up. She stood and threw her magazine on the floor.

"Rafael!"

"Que?" He lifted his arms.

She didn't say another word. She stormed past us and went downstairs, muttering "chatos" under her breath.

Celia returned holding a platter of deli meats and rice and beans she had heated in a Tupperware dish. I wondered what had taken her such a long time, nothing required cooking, but then I noticed her fingernails were painted with a fresh coat of green nail polish.

"Karina foi embora," said Rafael.

"Where did she go?"

"Não sei!"

Celia made a face, one that Rafael understood implicitly, and they both left it at that.

Celia had told me about her relationship with Rafael and Karina during our telephone conversations, but the reality of it hadn't crystallized for me until I saw them together in the flesh. Both Celia and Karina were protective of Rafael in their own ways. Karina wanted his body near her. If she could see him and feel him, then and only then did she trust he was with her. As soon as she lost sight of him, a panic was unearthed and she became erratic, accusing him of lying, of betrayal. As a result, they spent most of their time together, either painting graffiti or on top of each other around the apartment. Karina's protection appeared controlling, but really, it was Rafael who held the puppet strings in their relationship, knowing exactly when to pull away and when to give in. He was both the source of and the cure for her torment.

Celia's protection acted as a foil to Karina's. She liked being the one Rafael ran to when Karina was cocooned in solitude, focused solely on her art. She liked to cook for him, to give him advice, to understand the deeper parts of his ambitions in art, in family, in his desires to travel. It was like being offered a diamond from his mind that only she knew how to mine, or so she believed. She made sure he had enough to eat and drink. She asked him about his most recent photographs. She offered for him to come to the theater with her so that he could have a quiet space to work.

The irony was that all of the reasons Celia wanted to be close to Rafael were the same reasons I wanted to be close to Celia. Seeing her act this way with Rafael unnerved me, especially as he systematically ignored her to continue talking to me about the United States. I made a plate of food and tried to act friendly, if for nothing else, to make Celia happy.

"Do you live in New York City?" Rafael asked me, a sliver of ham dangling from his mouth.

"I don't. I live in Hartford, Connecticut."

"Hartford," he repeated, overextending the two "r"s. "Where is Hartford?"

"About two hours from New York City."

He laughed. "It is so close! Why don't you live in New York City?"

"Because my husband teaches there."

Celia interjected. "Her husband teaches at USP now."

"I always wanted to go to New York," Rafael continued. "I was a punk rocker and wanted to be a professional skateboarder. But then I broke my ankle." He wrapped his hand around his ankle as he said this. "So now I take photographs."

"A shame," I said and looked to Celia for direction, but she was patiently listening to Rafael.

"Do you go to New York often?" he asked.

"I have a couple times. I don't like cities very much." A black bird had landed on the cement wall. It picked at one of the white flowers growing over the side. "Times Square is my idea of a nightmare."

Celia laughed.

"You have to go downtown," said Rafael. "The Lower East Side."

"I'll keep that in mind." I offered him a slight smile, largely to make Celia comfortable. There was something about Rafael, a confident immaturity, that I was struggling with. But it was clear that Celia adored him, so I wanted to as well.

I noticed, on the rooftop two buildings to the right, a woman was taking a cold shower in a red bathing suit. We could have been on a porch in the country, had it not been for the high-rises around us. The only sound from the roof was the wind chime. Above us, I saw a man pruning his plants; he cut them with scissors, then allowed the dead heads to fall to the street.

"Did Rafael tell you about his photographs?" Celia asked. "He's very talented."

"He didn't," I said.

"Let me go get some," she offered, but Rafael resisted.

"Não, não."

Celia picked up the empty water pitcher.

"We need more water anyway," she said and began descending the stairs. "I'll be back."

Rafael reached under the couch and pulled out a wooden box filled with weed and papers. I watched him pinch the green pellets onto the creased paper and roll it between his fingers, expertly licking the edges as he rolled.

"What do you want to know about her?" he asked.

"Who?"

"You know."

"Karina?"

"Não." He lit the joint with a match. "Celia."

"I don't follow."

"I come home and she's on the floor curled up next to the telephone. She says she's talking to you."

"We call each other. It's nice to have a friend in São Paulo."

"Are you lonely?"

"Sometimes."

"Are you in love?"

"In love?" For some reason I didn't realize that he meant Celia.

"I love my husband," I said, and then knew I had misunderstood the implication. He put his feet on the table and crossed his arms over his chest.

"Meu Deus," he said and took a hit, the paper sparking red embers onto his lap.

We heard the clap of the office door and expected to see Celia with a new pitcher of water, but it was Karina. She walked up the mosaic steps with not a stitch of clothing on; only the white line from a bikini tan provided the illusion of covering. She carried a can of beer.

"Bom dia!" she said, brushing past us, and turned on the outdoor shower.

I looked at Rafael, expecting to see him shocked, perhaps even embarrassed, but instead he began to unbutton his pants. He tapped out the joint and threw off his sandals. When his pants were off and he was wearing only a small pair of yellow underwear, he rushed to her and into the water. He shrieked, "Nossa! Que fria!" By the time Celia returned with the pitcher in one hand and the other arm balancing Rafael's photography books, he was completely naked with Karina, each splashing the other and passing the beer back and forth.

"I should go," I said.

Celia looked horrified.

"Let me walk you to the door."

Downstairs it was silent and dim. The windows did not let in much light. Celia had a floral teacup, a sleeve of biscuits, and a laptop set up on the kitchen island. Plants grew in glass bottles on her windowsill, foggy with condensation, the roots finding traction against the smooth and hollow insides. I noticed Claudius was sleeping belly-up on a bed in the corner of the living room.

"We barely got to talk," she said. "It's my fault. I have a dead-line for a grant today. My attention was divided."

"That's all right," I said, and went to give Claudius a pat. He rolled onto his back and I rubbed his belly. "I feel bad for calling. It wasn't good timing."

"Don't," she said and took my hand. "You can always call."

That bit of reassurance was all I needed to melt away any insecurity I might have felt. She offered to make me a coffee but I told her I had to get back to the apartment. I didn't want to risk seeing Rafael and Karina again.

"I want to give you something," she said, and pulled a sealed envelope from underneath the laptop. "Wait a few days before you open it."

She handed me the letter and showed me out the door. I walked up the steep hill to the Madalena stop on the metro. As soon as I got inside the subway car I peeled open the envelope. Inside was a single piece of paper with a small, handwritten note:

Come to the beach with me?

Chapter Seventeen

At the end of the semester, the university gave you three weeks off before the start of the next term, in August. With you home all the time I told Celia that I wouldn't be able to talk on the phone. I didn't explain it like it was a secret, just that you and I would be spending more time out in the world. I was actually looking forward to it—we could go to museums, walk the park, take a trip to the coast. But you informed me that it wasn't a vacation. You would be doing research for an article the Provost wanted you to publish before you left USP.

Stacks of papers appeared on the kitchen table, like sedimentary rocks that had formed with the push of your hands. There was no room for me to eat lunch with you. I began to take my plate to the living room or the bedroom. You barely spoke. I tried to convince you to stop for a crossword or to walk with me to the grocery, but you buried yourself in your work. It was as though I was a ghost to you, someone who drifted by without so much as a shadow.

I soon learned it was a mistake to have created distance between me and Celia for the sake of your arrival. Your empty presence made me ache for Celia, an ache that metabolized behind my ribs. Involuntary functions—beat, breathe, beat, breathe—shuddered to a crawl, as if a claw was grabbing at my tongue from the inside of my throat, dragging me to the floor. I'm alone, I thought. I'm alone, I thought again.

Meanwhile, Marta reacted to your every need. She tended to your water glass and coffee mug, picked up your socks and shoes, swept the floor around you. I had not seen you and Marta interact for such sustained periods of time. The way you so easily connected with each other, so effortlessly interacted and abated each other's intensity, made me cower.

When she brought you a coffee or water you thanked her and grinned with delight. She cooked you lunch, and you remarked on how her vegetables were the perfect firmness, or how she always picked the sweetest mangoes, or how you loved the way she made rice with yellow onions and salt.

"Can you show Linda how to make this rice, Marta?" you said, rice stuck between your teeth, rice covering the kitchen table. "It's delicious."

I tried to return to painting, but it was impossible for me to concentrate knowing you and Marta were in the other room together. This feeling swept through me, a wind of doubt, that you appreciated her more than you did me. I wondered if you two spoke in whispers while I ate lunch in the other room. I imagined opening the bathroom door to find you behind her, pants at your ankles, Marta's stomach pressed against the sink. Maybe she tells you that I'm a recluse while you go to work. Maybe she tells you I want to be left alone. Why don't you see me? I thought. I'm standing right here, a pain growing inside my heart. Why don't you see me? And yet you didn't hear— your head remained bowed over the paperwork, your attention only open when Marta offered a café com leite.

Then, one day, I went to the kitchen to pour a glass of iced tea, and noticed a long, curly hair spread across the counter. I picked it up and realized that the hair was not mine, it was not Marta's, it certainly wasn't yours. It was Celia's. Marta had just cleaned the kitchen, so how was it possible that she had missed the hair beside the sink? Of course, I didn't think all that much of it at the time (though it did feel peculiar—how did Celia's hair get into the apartment anyhow? Had it been on my blouse? Had I brushed it out of my own hair?). And then, a few days later, I found a balled-up note in the trash. It was Celia's phone number. I had kept that small scrap of paper tucked into the corner of my purse. How had it ended up there? But what perturbed me most was the can of palmitos. I opened up the cabinet and the labels stared back at me: *Celialana*. Really? Out of nowhere Marta chose a new brand. *Celia-lana*. These events alone wouldn't amount to anything, but for the addition of one after another.

Old habits returned. Instincts that did not rise above but sank deep down into petty retribution. I played a game. When you would get up to go to the bathroom, I would sneak into the kitchen and take a piece of paper from the top of one of your stacks and slip it into the middle. It would only be a few minutes before you began to flounder, searching for the paper, flipping over notepads and textbooks.

"Linda!" you'd shout. "Did I leave a piece of paper in the bathroom?"

I'd return, "No, dear!"

A few more minutes would pass and I'd come to your rescue, help you sort through the stacks, until I found the exact page you were looking for.

"Thank you," you'd say and give me a kiss on the top of my hand.

How helpful I was!

I couldn't do it too frequently or else it would seem obvious. But I did different combinations a few times a day. Put a piece of paper on the floor under the table. Rearranged the order of documents. Took your good pen into the bedroom. One day I decided to have a cafezinho and a pão de queijo for lunch downstairs, so I took a reference list with me. I placed my purse on the café table and realized the tip of the list had dipped into my coffee. I wiped it with a napkin from the canister, but they were flimsy wax sheets; the coffee soaked easily into the paper. I was sure the jig was up. Of course you'd notice the stain. You'd smell the fried bolinho. I hurried upstairs expecting to see you flummoxed, in need of the document, but you were on the sofa taking a nap. I carefully returned it to the folder.

Marta saw everything. She watched me every time I tiptoed into the kitchen, and I watched her watch me, knowing she couldn't say anything. Should I have confronted her about the messages or shouldn't I? The question plagued me. The more I considered it, the more I began to worry that these weren't harmless hints at all, but a plan she'd concocted to sabotage my relationship with Celia. The messages could have been part of a scheme to expose us. But what could I say to Marta? Are you trying to ruin a relationship I won't admit to having? I was growing restless. I tried to call Celia, but she didn't answer. I tried again—still no answer. I woke up one morning and had a terrible idea.

I can say now, in my defense, that growth is a process of progression and regression. Many phrases come to mind that don't describe my particular version of victory and sabotage, especially when it came to Marta. Two steps forward, one step back. Shed leaves to grow new ones. What I mean to say is, all my insecurities had scattered to hidden recesses, like ants without a colony, but once they found one another again, my hive brain pointed toward Marta. I had hidden the gold key to Marta's room behind my jewelry box. It was so small and light, I barely felt it in the palm of my hand.

As soon as I hitched the door open, I could smell the sweet-bitter incense she had stubbed against the wooden shelf, the ash smudged in blue-gray streaks. Her closet was big enough to fit shelves on one wall, a crate with a small television and a radio, and a small children's bed. On the shelves she kept a pressed gardenia propped between her St. Christopher the Divine candle and a troll doll with a wisp of green hair and an emerald belly button. The objects were nestled, hugged in place, as though they'd been there for decades. There were two books: a softcover Bible and a copy of *One Hundred Years of Solitude,* the pages yellowed with age. Her bedsheets were bubblegum pink with cartoon cats all over. I lay down, my legs stretched out the door. In the corner of the ceiling she had tacked a poster of Jesus Christ nailed to the cross, head slung, in the same spot I had kept a magazine clipping of George Michael as a teenager.

What was I hoping to find? A doll with pins stuck in the eyes, as Melinda had suggested? A wall covered in photographs of me and Celia? I felt the soft indent in the center of her mattress, the rough texture from the line-dried linen. She had nothing to hide. I was the one who was hiding. I locked the door behind me without evidence of anything, except, perhaps, my own delusions, which disturbed me even more. I didn't want to go down this dark path again. I didn't want my healing to come at Marta's expense.

Chapter Eighteen

"Don't hate me," you said. It wasn't the best way to start the day. I was standing in front of our bathroom mirror, observing the red creases that ran across my face from where I had slept on the pillow.

"I don't hate you. What is it?"

"I told Eduardo that you would go shopping with Melinda today."

"Okay, maybe I do hate you. Why on earth would you do that?"

Apparently Melinda had been asking her husband since our dinner when they were going to see us again. She said she felt a kinship with me. I pressed one of the lines on my face to try to rub it away.

"Couldn't she have called me?" I said. "Why did she ask the Provost to ask you?"

You shrugged.

"I know why. She knows that if she asked me directly, I would find an excuse not to go."

"Maybe." You paused. "So will you go?"

"I honestly do hate that you're asking me this."

I could see through the mirror your big, helpless smile. Maybe I was feeling guilty for how I had been acting, but it was too difficult to say no.

"Fine," I said. "But I'm not buying anything."

I met Melinda on Rua Oscar Freire, a sumptuous display of healthy trees and women in athletic pants strolling with their small dogs. Melinda toted me around as she tried on gowns for her upcoming charity benefit.

"It's to raise money for the Amazon," she explained, half unzipped in a white satin dress. Her back was thin and had many scars where moles had been removed. "Did you know that slavery still exists in the cane fields up north? It's horrendous. We are fortunate to live in São Paulo."

"We are," I said and looked at the glittering gown hugging her body. "Some more fortunate than others."

She wrapped her arm around her back and pulled the zipper up halfway. The dress was too small. She wiggled to pull down the hem and eyed the mirror with a pout.

"What do you think?" she asked and turned to me. I sat on a leather sofa with a Persian cat curled up on my lap.

"It's beautiful," I told her, though I could tell she was holding her breath to cinch in her stomach. She called in the direction of two young store clerks, who stood to the side at a discreet distance, waiting for her decision.

"The hem is too long," she said, and they dashed over, dropped to their knees, and began to pin as she admired her waistline.

When they were done, they unzipped her, and she allowed the dress to fall to her ankles. It was odd to see her so bare, wearing nothing but a pair of large beige undergarments.

"They're going to hem the dress by this evening," she said. "In the meantime, can I take you to lunch?"

I was starving—I could taste the hunger on my breath—and so I agreed. We found a restaurant on the same block. On the way, Melinda noticed a woman walking her dog and said, "That's an ugly dog," loud enough that I'm sure the woman heard.

"Melinda!" I said. "Don't say that."

I startled myself with how stern I sounded. Melinda looked startled too.

"It's just—don't you see how that could hurt the woman's feelings?"

"What does it matter?" she said, clearly offended. "I'm never going to see her or that dog again anyway."

I decided that I was going to drink wine at lunch. As much wine as they would bring me. We sat at a table next to a large, second-floor window that overlooked the expensive shops below. The windows reflected harshly against the afternoon sun, so Melinda asked the hostess if we could close the blinds. As the hostess walked away, I tried to mouth to her "Desculpa," but she didn't see me.

"I'm so glad we have this quality time together," Melinda said. "Our husbands always see each other, and I thought, Why not us? Why shouldn't we have this luxury?"

I picked up the menu. "Do you want to drink wine? Or is it too early?"

She pretended to look at an imaginary watch on her wrist. "It's just the time."

The waiter came by, and she ordered a bottle of white wine and barely enough food. I ordered a cod sandwich. When he returned with our lunch, in an attempt at small talk, I asked Melinda how long she and Eduardo had been married.

"Almost thirty years. Thirty years at the end of September."

"That's nice," I said. "How did you meet?"

"I was his student." She laughed to herself. "He was married when I met him. Not many people know that. His wife had a miscarriage and was suffering from psychiatric problems. She would wake up in the middle of the night and hit him, tell him he was evil and that she hated him." She ashed her cigarette underneath the table. "At the time I was young and so madly in love. What did I know? I thought his wife was horrible. I begged him to leave her. I would do anything for him, in the bedroom, in the kitchen, whatever he wanted. In exchange he taught me literature and poetry and history. So he left her. I was thrilled. I kissed the divorce papers."

She stopped speaking for a moment, seemingly to calibrate how much to say next. I kept drinking my wine.

"I love Eduardo. People change, people make mistakes. He and his ex-wife would have divorced if I was in the picture or not." She pushed a piece of lettuce to the edge of her plate and continued. "When my daughter was a baby, Eduardo worked all the time. I was terribly bored. There was a man who came by to water our orchids. Eduardo was very specific about these orchids. He thought that if *I* watered them they would die. So we had a man who specialized in orchids come to spray them twice a week. He was young—maybe my age at the time, or younger. He watched the same telenovela that I watched, so we talked about the episodes every week. He would tell me about the other gardens he tended, about his own orchids, about the physiology of trees. We developed a close bond. At least, I thought so. Now I think maybe it was part of his job to keep lonely housewives company."

She dabbed the corner of her mouth as she said this, as if the thought left a bad taste in her mouth.

"I fantasized about what our relationship would be like. How he and I would have a small house in the country with our own garden. I even thought about the carrots, how he'd bring them in and leave them by the sink, and I would rinse off the dirt and chop them into a salad. I thought about what kind of father he would be. It was all so unlikely, but I prayed that it would happen. I really believed that it might." She paused. "Do you think I am silly?"

I didn't think it was silly. In fact, I wished I could meet this version of Melinda.

"No, I don't think you're silly," I said. "Imagination is a gift." She grinned and asked the waiter for another bottle of wine.

I assumed that Melinda told me this story because she wanted me to know that she had a tender side, that she wasn't built entirely from vinegar. At moments in her life, I could find drops of honey, if only I cared to look.

But it was becoming increasingly difficult for me to concentrate. The alcohol had buoyed my confidence, making my impulses steam with urgency. I wanted to ask her about something specific, something that had been plaguing me since the day I met her. I didn't care if she would take out her aggression on me, and I knew that, by this point, your relationship with the Provost was strong enough that he wouldn't take his aggression out on you.

"Melinda, can I say something?"

"Of course. I would love it if you did."

"Those things you said about Marta, you know they aren't true, right?"

She cocked her head to the side, as if she didn't remember what I was talking about.

I continued. "You told me, or at least insinuated, that Marta had been scheming against people she worked for. You told me that she had caused illness in that French professor."

"I don't think those were my exact words."

"They were. And the worst part is, I believed you. Not outright, but the stories clung to my memory, and I realized I was associating Marta with them, whether I knew it or not."

She took a sip of wine. "I think you're reading too much into it. I was merely repeating what I had heard as a warning to you."

"I want you to promise you won't say those things about Marta again."

She shifted in her seat and let out a laugh. I could feel the wine buzzing on my tongue.

"I mean it." I picked up my fork and pointed it at her. "Don't tell those stories about Marta again. Don't talk about her at all."

"Okay," she said. "You're upset, I can tell."

"Just say it, so I know. You won't talk about Marta again."

"Fine," she said. "I won't tell those stories again."

I knew I wasn't going to get any more out of her. "I appreciate it," I said and took a last bite of my sandwich. We finished the bottle of wine and she left her food virtually untouched. Melinda paid for my taxi home and told me she would let me know how the charity event went.

I had only been gone for two, maybe three hours, but when I returned the apartment was empty. Only a stack of books and papers remained on the kitchen table. Something else was missing too. I didn't identify it at first—I only felt the shift in energy, the lingering feeling that something was out of place. Then I saw it: my painting, the one that Marta had hung above the kitchen table. It had been taken down. It was propped against the bottom cabinets, its back facing out, so that all I could see was my inscription: LINDA, 2004.

For a moment I thought, believed, that a robber had broken into the apartment and he was stockpiling his loot. I held my breath, frozen. The latch on the door opened.

"Linda, you're home," you said, more surprised than I was, and put a bag of coxinha down on the counter. The grease seeped through the wax paper, forming transparent spots.

"How was it?"

"How was what?" I answered.

"Jardins. With Melinda."

"Oh. It was fine. She shopped. Then we had lunch."

You walked to the kitchen table and glanced at the painting on the floor, but acted like it was nothing, like it could have been a pair of shoes you left there earlier.

"Dennis," I said.

"Yes?"

"Why is my painting on the floor?"

Your eyes lowered.

"I meant to put it back before you got home."

You tried to fix it; you picked her up by the frame and tried to put her back on the wall. But the look on my face must have told you otherwise.

"I'm sorry," you said and rested her on the table.

"Why was it on the floor?"

"I don't know how to say this without upsetting you."

That will only upset me more, I thought. "Just tell me."

You fumbled to find the words to explain it. I can't remember another time when I'd seen your discomfort manifest so visibly—you crossed your arms tight over your chest and kept your eyes on the floor; shook your head and started and stopped sentences halfway through.

"Her eyes," you said. "They follow me." You picked up the painting to demonstrate. "See? She's looking at you."

I observed the painting: her legs crooked over the bathtub ledge, her stomach cresting from the water's surface, her eyes and parted mouth facing the viewer. I remembered the painstaking layers that it took to proportion her legs so that they looked strong and feminine.

"I don't see it," I said. "What do you mean?"

It started when you began researching at home. You'd look up with a thought and notice the woman looking down at you.

The first time you stared back, trying to will your mind into believing that it was an illusion, that it's not possible for a painting to stare. But she was, you said. You changed seats—across the table, catty-corner, even with your back to the wall—but you could still feel her eyes upon you, even when you didn't look up to see her.

"It began to affect my work. But what was I supposed to do? Go to another room? This is the only place with enough space for me to work."

One day, when I wasn't around, you took her down from the wall. Just for a few minutes. And when you put her back up, somehow her gaze had adjusted. She stopped looking, and you could work freely again.

"That fixed it for a while, but then it came back. A few minutes wasn't enough. I needed her down there for longer." You paused. "I'm sorry, Linda. You know I love your paintings."

Perhaps I should have taken your explanation for what it was: that you needed to focus and the painting was a distraction. But the painting meant so much more to me than that. It was emblematic of a transformation, of a skill that I had taught myself when I truly thought I had no skills. It was special to me. I saw Celia, my muse, my inspiration, in that painting. I saw myself in that painting. I was deeply hurt.

I yelled at you for what felt like an eternity, accused you of disrespecting me, of pressuring me to meet with Melinda, and meanwhile spitting on the one thing I was proud of. I told you that I thought you had changed, that your relationship with the Provost had turned you into an opportunist, that I didn't recognize the man I had married. When I finished you were dumbstruck, vacant, a sand castle washed away by the tide.

"It's not true," you said. "I'm not explaining myself well."

"It is true. Even if you don't know it, it is."

I closed myself in the bedroom. You tried to come in and

console me, but I pushed you away. You tried again, and again, until I asked you to leave the apartment, and you agreed to go to the library.

I ran my hands under cool water, lay down on the bed, and watched the ceiling turn.

When you came home from the library, I wouldn't be there, and the flowers you bought me would go rotten before I returned, the water green and the stems black, the wrinkled petals fallen in a perfect circle around the vase.

Chapter Nineteen

Something broke inside me after our fight. Not to pieces, but a pop, the first sound before a firework crackles. It was a culmination of everything that had led up to that moment. The flame started in my chest and then ruptured, so that I was turned inside out, chest spread over my clavicles and around my shoulder blades. I was a burst woman when I called Celia and she finally answered. I asked if she could come over, and Celia appeared downstairs within the hour. I'll call this new woman "L," a woman who rushed out the door, arms flung open when Celia arrived. L met her out on the street and the tears followed. Celia embraced L and said she'd take her to the shore, where L could rejuvenate, just as her note had promised. She explained that she too needed to escape for a few days, that her house was filled with toxic energy, and that's why she hadn't returned L's calls. She needed to be near the ocean.

L agreed without question. She ran upstairs to pack her bag while Celia waited for her outside. L uncovered the roll of reais you kept tucked in the back of the closet. L tossed the money, bathing suits, dresses, and a toothbrush into a backpack and met Celia at the bottom of the stairs. She left you a note:

> *I left for the beach.*
> > *Love,*
> > > *Linda*

They did the same at Celia's apartment, then left for the bus station, where they boarded a six-hour bus to Paraty, a small coastal village just south of Rio de Janeiro.

How is escape quantified? In hours, in distance, by the levity of a hole? How far did L need to run before she felt—yes, of course, I've escaped. Wouldn't she always worry that she'd be found the second she forgot that she was gone? Even if L could erase her memory against the sweeping hillside farms she watched through the bus window, a small piece of her would always worry that they hadn't gone far enough.

But at that moment, now hours outside of São Paulo, the cityscape no longer visible in the skyline, L wasn't worried at all. Celia pressed her forehead against the glass and described to her the various techniques for planting trees on mountains. She pointed to a group of perfectly lined trees planted on a diagonal down a mountain.

"If you plant trees in rows that point straight down the mountain, rainwater will wash up the roots and unplant the trees." She looked at L directly. "That's why they plant them diagonally. Isn't that incredible?"

L took the bag of puff chips from her lap and crunched them loudly.

"The tree would go tumbling down the mountain?"

Celia took one too and bit it inch by inch with her two front teeth.

"Yes. I guess it would."

The bus stopped at a roadside market lit by the moonlight. It was late, maybe ten or eleven at night. The market housed giant hares in pens out front. Celia struck a match to reveal them cuddled together in a corner, their red eyes flat reflections in the light. L and Celia huddled too, and whispered to each other how sweet the animals were, keeping warm with their sisters. They went to the restroom and L listened to the sounds Celia made in the adjacent stall, hoped that she could time her body to match Celia's in the way women close to each other can. They met at the sinks, exchanged smiles in the mirrors.

One method to convince your mind that your body has traveled far enough is to sleep and hope that the dreams take you farther from, not closer to, your starting point. Nothing is worse than a dream that traps you, rats you out, reveals the fearful detail. When sleep doesn't work, a second method is alcohol. Celia had packed a warm flask of tequila, which stung and scratched the backs of their throats as they passed it back and forth. They laughed through it. L, in many ways, had reverted to teenage primitivism, and Celia had the tricks of a high school rebel. She pulled a cigarette from the center of her bra and they each took a drag and exhaled into a plastic bottle. When they arrived at the hostel in the middle of the night, a short walk from the center of Paraty, Celia opened the bottle and smoke drifted out into the twilight.

A sleeping man in a floral tunic guarded the wooden gates that led to a small camping ground and the hostel cabins. The hostel room had a cement floor and a bunk bed, a fan plugged into the single outlet, and a miniature refrigerator in the corner. Celia pulled a lava lamp from her duffel bag and plugged it into the fan's socket.

"It will help with the mosquitos," she said. The lava particles had broken apart in travel so the purple light refracted around the room. From outside, all the other windows glowed yellow against the deep blue night, while theirs hummed with a soft purple.

L and Celia walked into town to look for a restaurant with live music. The streets were made of large stones and deep divots. The difference between Paraty's tourists and the natives was most evident in their walk. The locals glided over the stone pathways with ease—mountain, jungle, and ocean ease—while the rest of us needed to watch each step or risk falling.

This land wasn't built for visitors, but it burned at night for them. With mud-stained skirt hems and necks and wrists adorned by green and purple stones, the locals captivated the tourists, cajoling us into bar fronts by offering pizza and Heineken beer. With Celia next to her, L could detect the ruses. She avoided the temptations of American culture that had flopped its tentacles into this fishing town, declined each advance for an American quesadilla or American whiskey, instead opting for the local cachaça, Gabriela, and baskets of coxinha. Celia stared adoringly, both soft and vain, a look that only a mentor can have for her pupil.

Celia and L returned to the hostel room, and Celia climbed into the top bunk without removing her shoes. The sleeping accommodations were tenuous. If one leg moved an inch, the metal frame rattled. L folded herself into the thin wool blanket and watched as Celia dropped articles of clothing to the floor, first one sandal, then the second, her blouse, a bra, a brass necklace, a pair of jeans. L waited, listened, tried to imagine if Celia slept on her back or on her stomach, chin and breasts pressed against the mattress that separated the two of them. At one point in the night, Celia got up to drink a bottle of water from the minifridge, and L wondered if she would forget which bed was hers. She didn't. She climbed the metal ladder and the frame swayed with each step.

After Celia lay back down, only the insects could be heard. Eventually L was certain Celia had fallen back asleep, and so she too slept, and woke up not as a woman drifting outside her body, but as a woman who more deeply understood herself.

It's me, Dennis. It's still me. I had dreamt about this escape for a long time, a place where I could collect the parts that I actually like about myself, and leave behind the rest. I was ready to grow. And I now know, this type of growth can only be learned through an emotional apprenticeship from another woman who has learned the same.

Chapter Twenty

I woke the next morning to an engine revving outside our window. Celia was already awake and in the shower, and so I opened the wooden shutters to find a teenage boy playing with his motorbike in the camping ground. He sped a little and then slid the tires to kick up dirt onto a stray dog that was barking and chasing after him.

"Good morning," I heard from behind me and turned to find Celia standing naked in the doorframe, drying her body with a towel.

"I thought we could go to Trindade today," she said. "It's an hour bus ride through the mountains, but it's worth it." She sat down on the toilet and kept talking through the door. "I slept terribly! What a horrible bed that is. We'll sleep on the beach."

Once she'd dressed she went outside to ask for a cigarette from the boy on the motorbike. She had left hairs in the sink and a swipe of blue mascara on the towel. I hadn't realized before how messy she was, but part of me took pleasure in tidying up after her. I gathered up her hairs and tossed them into the toilet, then cleaned the sink and the counter. I wiped my body down with a wet hand cloth and chose a dress in a color similar to Celia's, green with small white daisies all over. She waited for me, swinging in the hammock strung on our porch, one leg dangling off the edge. We crossed the street to a café and drank cafezinhos, ate bread with ham and soft, tangy cheese baked into the top.

To escape, in essence, is to forget. Maybe it was easier because Celia never mentioned São Paulo. She hardly spoke about the past or the future, unless it was so distant that it had managed to return to the present. I had forgotten, as she and I ate our pastries and sipped our coffees, watching two gray cats twist in a pool of sunlight, that eventually I had to go back home. I had forgotten that you might be driven crazy by now, perhaps involving the Provost, perhaps involving the police. In reality, you were locked in anger. You made no phone calls, mentioned my escape to no one, not even to the clock on the wall. Every second that passed you made a choice to forget, which is not the same as actually forgetting.

On the first night of my escape, you returned home from work and found the note I'd left. The apartment made no noise, except for the occasional tick of a pipe behind the sink. You sat frozen at the kitchen table until you could assemble your thoughts into tangible shapes, shapes that you could cobble together. An hour passed. You investigated the bedroom and noticed the missing duffel bag, the thin gaps in the closet. You deduced that I had enough clothing for a few days at most. You noticed the box of jewelry and photographs left behind. She would never leave without this photograph, you thought, holding a picture of my mother in her garden. You sat on the edge of the mattress and wrestled with the dimming light.

Your worry morphed into frustration. You drank a can of beer. You splashed cold water on your face. You lay awake in bed, cursing me, cursing my neglect, and then, after a few hours of contemplation, you slept. You woke up the next morning resolute, thinking she would return because, frankly, where else would she go?

Celia stood from her chair, paid the woman at the cashier, and we walked to the center of town. She held on to the hem of my dress, and I rested my hand on her shoulder, gleefully following her to the bus station.

We were the last to board the packed bus, and so Celia took a seat with a young surfer in the first row. I had to fend for myself in the back of the bus, where one seat had opened across from a boy and his grandmother. The boy was covered in white boils, even on his eyelids. He seemed to understand his sympathy-evoking condition, and so he caused such a commotion that it was impossible not to look at him. His main performance was the bus dance. He took great pleasure in mirroring the bus's movements, revving and crashing every time we stopped, started, turned, or veered. His grandmother, a stout woman whose waist collapsed over two seats, watched him with amusement. She clapped every time her grandson faked a big fall or pretended the bus had exploded. The performance continued when we left the main street and the bus hobbled onto the mountain. Palm leaves brushed the open windows and sometimes hit passengers in the face. The boy found this incredibly funny. He mocked the creaky bus by impersonating an old man with a cane, one hand on his hip, bent over, the other hand wobbling out front. Some passengers gave him coins. But when we reached the top of the mountain, the grandmother straightened her face and told the boy to sit down. He listened. He buckled his seatbelt and tucked the coins in his pocket.

The bus clung to the mountainside as we circled inches from a cliff, the driver shifting gears across angled turns. Some of these passengers were on a commute home from work. The driver picked up children along the way who had finished school. I looked to the front of the bus to make eye contact with Celia, hoping to find a mutual glimpse of astonishment, but Celia laughed, unconcerned with the bronzed surfer.

The bus arrived at Trindade, and most passengers disembarked to the right, toward the center of town. I began to follow the crowd, but Celia stopped me. The surfer had given her directions to the ocean. He pointed through a small expanse of open grassland. She kissed him on the cheek and repeated the directions back to him, thanked him again with a kiss on the other cheek, and left him at the stop.

We walked through grassland, underneath a canopy of spindly branches, until the end of the path revealed a crescent shoreline. The morning had brought us sunshine, but since then clouds had edged into the afternoon. I could see the moon sitting close to the horizon, a white pastel sphere peeking through the blue expanse, kicking up waves against the coast. I was transfixed by the repeated force—boom, slap, boom, slap—crashing against the black rocks jutting from the inlet. Water on stone on water.

"I liked that surfer," Celia said.

"What did you two talk about?"

"My mother. His parents are Lebanese too." She drew a figure eight in the sand with her sandal. "I should have invited him to come with us."

She started toward the other side of the beach and waved for me to keep moving. I joined her, and we walked across a stream to the base of a mountain. Celia tossed her sandals on the dirt shoreline—the soft jungle soil would have swallowed them whole on our hike. We went barefoot, Celia in front, the ocean at our side, the tangled rainforest surrounding us. I smelled the viscous honey drops, heard the vibrato of dragonfly wings, felt the chilly breeze from the oceanside. When I looked up to share in this glory with Celia, I realized that she had climbed well ahead and was stopped, waiting, arms crossed and looking down at me.

"What's taking so long?" she said.

I apologized, hurried up, and she turned and kept hiking.

I thought maybe this was just a hiccup. What could I possibly have done to bother her?

A toucan flew over our heads and landed high on a tree branch, so I craned my head over the edge to look for him. Celia scolded me for being reckless. I took a drink from a halved bamboo stalk. Celia commented on how exhausted I looked.

"Maybe you should exercise more."

"I exercise," I said.

"I'm kidding," she answered, her back already to me. "Don't be so serious all the time."

She led us to a cove with gray boulders breaking from the water's surface. They looked like the backs of giant tortoise-shells. Other hikers had stopped too to sunbathe. We waded through the water until we found our own rock to spread across, the porous surface warming our skin. We stretched our bodies there, enjoying the passing sunrays that peeked through and dodged behind the clouds. I could feel, though, that Celia wasn't relaxed. She'd turn to one side and then the other, sigh heavily, until she roused, sat up, and began to throw broken shells into the schools of fish hovering against the tide.

Finally she spoke.

"I want to tell you something, but I'm afraid you won't like it," she said.

"You don't have to tell me anything."

She paused. I thought maybe she wouldn't.

"Is it about our trip?" I asked.

"No," she said. "It's about why I left."

Her body had slumped. She picked at a bit of white moss and threw it into the water.

"Rafael and I . . ." Her words slowed; anxiety pricked at my stomach. I then realized that her sudden change in attitude had nothing to do with me.

"We're in love."

"For how long?"

"Several months. Maybe even a year."

"Does Karina know?"

"No. Not really. She knows, but she doesn't know."

"How far has this gone?"

Her brows crimped. "What do you mean?"

"Have you had sex with him?"

"Yes," she said. I turned my back and looked toward the horizon.

The trip had been an escape for her too. She told me that she and Rafael had known each other far longer than he and Karina had, a point she made as an excuse, a "pass." He met Karina because they were both graffiti artists, but their love didn't have the foundation in trust, the longevity, that she had with him. The love affair began with simple gestures. They would share meals together when Karina bartended at night. Sometimes Celia would sit with Rafael when he was fresh out of the shower, covering her eyes when it was time for him to change, until one day he told her she didn't have to, and she blushed when he stood naked in front of her, not like a brother but like a Roman statue, laughing with delight.

"Did you make love then?" I asked her, but she denied it. They made love after many months, after many conversations and nights spent alone. He formed a habit of falling asleep in bed with Celia and setting an alarm for an hour before Karina was due to arrive home from work.

"The nights we couldn't spend together were torture," she said. "Sometimes I would wake in the middle of the night just to peek into his bedroom and see him sleeping."

The problems started when one night he didn't wake up and Karina found him curled underneath Celia's sheets. He tried to convince Karina that he had sleepwalked—that he had gotten up to go to the bathroom and wandered into the wrong room. But she refused to believe him. She became volatile; she rifled through their drawers when they left; she asked their friends to report back to her if they ever saw them together.

"Please don't tell anyone," Celia said to me.

"Who would I tell?"

"I don't know. If anyone can find us, it's Karina."

I told her that she should stop seeing him, that it was the most logical solution, that he was young and impulsive and that he would leave both of them in the end. Desperation consumed her.

"He's an artist. Karina doesn't give him space." She stood up and began to pace across the rock. The tide was rising—I could see the waterlines on the other rocks had disappeared. The hikers had begun to pack their bags and shimmy off. Even the fish found shelter within the kelp.

"Don't get upset," I said. "I do like Rafael. I worry about your friendship with Karina."

"He's everything to me. More than my friendship with Karina," she said, massaging her temples. "I would give up my life for him."

I didn't respond to that—I assumed she was being dramatic. I suggested we return to the trail; the water was too deep to walk across. She agreed, collected her things, and jumped off the side, while I found a safe foothold to lower myself down.

We swam on our backs, holding our packs up with one hand, and hiked the muddy trail back to the beach. It should have been a warning to me that perhaps I wasn't the only stranger she had grown close to in her life, that maybe I wasn't as singular a love as I had assumed. Even a tanned surfer on a bus to Trindade could instantly become a confidant, a dog she fostered from the favela streets could become her best friend, an American woman wearing a shower cap could become a travel companion. Yet these were the qualities that attracted me to Celia. Her fearless compassion. Her loyalty to the unknown. They were the same things that attracted Rafael to her.

"I need a beer," Celia said and suggested we eat on the beach rather than wait until we got back to Paraty. We found a small restaurant set back from the shore. Neither of us brought up the conversation about Rafael—we spoke only about what we wanted to eat and drink. It was better that way. We ordered a basket of fried fish and beer, and Celia squeezed lime all over our fish. A short rain broke from the sky, dripping off the palm leaves above us. We waited for it to stop before we made our way back to the road.

The bus stop was much less crowded on the way up the mountain; most people had left before the storm. Celia and I sat next to each other in the back. She rested her head against the bus window and dozed. And I—I couldn't stop thinking about her and Rafael. To me he seemed so young, so self-interested, which was likely insecurity, but he masked that insecurity with bold acts of rebellion. I pictured them together behind closed doors in her apartment, listening for Karina to return home, Rafael grabbing at Celia's body like a clumsy dog wrestling with a toy, unsure of how to approach her first. And Celia, coaxing him with the flick of her tongue. Could she really be in love? I found it impossible.

I didn't want to think about it anymore. I focused my attention on something else, anything else, which of course led me back to you. I wondered if it had been a mistake to follow Celia here. I thought about one Saturday morning early on in our days in Brazil, when you promised that you would stay home with me, that the university would be a distant concern, despite impending deadlines and exams and essays to grade. I slept better than I had since we first arrived, drifting into consciousness, hovering in a calm cocoon. The sound of faucet water flooded my dreams. I woke to the smell of a freshly peeled orange. You were already up and at the bathroom sink, a pile of rinds where you normally lay. I pulled a pillow over my face and let my breath warm the cotton stuffing. A deeper noise broke through, rattling deep and muffled. Thwap. Thwap. Thwap.

"Dennis. Do you hear that?"

You didn't say anything. You had a toothbrush in your mouth.

"Dennis," I said again, this time into open air.

"It sounds like trees breaking," you said.

The shutters on our window were tied together with a chiffon scarf, woven through the metal handles. I shimmied over and untied it with a pull. The noise boomed into the room. I kneeled so I could see just over the window ledge.

"They're building something inside the soccer stadium."

The pile drivers moved primitively, consistent and slow, like a pack of long-necked dinosaurs feeding in a dusty pool. I stood to get a better view. "They're digging a massive hole where the soccer field used to be."

The scarf lay tangled beneath my feet. I picked it up and retied the window shut.

"How long do you think this will last?"

"I don't know," you said. "I guess it depends how big they need the hole to be."

"Very funny. I wonder what it's for."

"I hope an ice-skating rink." You put a hand to your chin. "Or no—a helicopter pad. We could spend the day skiing in the Alps and come back to Brazil before Monday."

"I could go home to Hartford while you're at the university."

"I'd take you to Paris. Or Anguilla. Anywhere in the world."

"Anywhere?" I thought for a moment. "I still think I'd like to go home."

"Okay. We'll go home. And then we'll go to Pluto."

"What if I stayed? What if I didn't want to go to Pluto?" I said this, though I knew I could never stay without you.

"I'd miss you. I don't think I could go without you."

I made us breakfast: bowls of Cheerios with nonperishable milk. You sat with a newspaper across your lap and a coffee mug in your hand. We could hear the hard echo from metal banging against metal.

"Look at this." You pointed to the newspaper. "Two thousand people lost their homes in that hurricane on the coast."

"That's terrible," I said. "I don't know how to respond to bad news anymore."

You folded up the paper and tucked it underneath the ceramic bowl. "Hey. Let's go to the park today. It's beautiful outside."

We went to the bedroom together and you undressed me gingerly, pulled my dress over my lifted arms, and pressed me onto the mattress. You were careful, as you are, to kiss my neck and my breasts and my stomach before you removed my underwear and entered me. When you were done, you collapsed and kissed me on the shoulder, grinning so hard I could feel your teeth poke through.

Chapter Twenty-one

Celia and I spent the following day on a harborside beach. Blue and red and yellow fishing boats bobbed against the forested horizon. We had only beach wraps to lie on and the sand was hard, so Celia used my stomach as a headrest while she napped.

Behind us a weathered man cooked slabs of pork shoulder and ribs on a cast-iron grill. Charcoal and salt mist filled the air. The beach was quiet, but for an occasional gull overhead, diving to catch a silver fish in the dark water.

We'd been gone for two days. I imagined your face, blank with worry, withdrawn from teaching, reaching for the ringing telephone. The thought made me sink with guilt.

Celia roused and shook my foot.

"Do you want to go in the water?"

I told her I'd go in a bit and watched her walk into the cold ocean and plunge, her long hair pouring behind her.

Night two of my escape, you heated a bowl of lasagna that Marta left you and sat in your chair at the kitchen table as if I were there too, but then moved to the living room to get away from the absence of me. You wanted badly to pretend my leaving hadn't bothered you. You washed your bowl and left it on the side of the sink. You stayed up late organizing papers and listening to Joni Mitchell. You woke up several times in the night; thoughts of my return pushed you into consciousness. But each time you managed to squash the possibility and fell asleep again.

Celia placed her wet hair on my stomach and closed her eyes. At the far side of the beach, two teenage boys had arrived on bicycles. One I recognized as the boy on the motorbike that Celia had met the previous morning.

"Oi!" he yelled, recognizing Celia, and waved his hand through the air.

Celia shielded her brow from the sun and asked me who it was.

"It's the boy with the motorbike. You smoked a cigarette with him."

They ambled over the sand with their bicycles. They were both sinewy and eager, their bodies burning faster than life could feed them. The motorbiker's name was Victor. Victor wore a dark braid down his back and a nervous smile. The friend, Felipe, had matured more than Victor—his arms and shoulders were broader, the beginnings of a beard darkened his chin and neck—but he chuckled and squeaked at the sight of us.

Celia barely lifted an eyelid, but they began chatting with her instantly. I understood a few phrases: How did we like the hostel, had we met the owner's son, he was a friend of theirs, they lived nearby, sometimes they camped at the hostel, they planned to go fishing at dusk, was this our first time in Paraty, would we be out at the bars tonight?

Celia interrupted them. "My friend doesn't speak Portuguese."

"It's okay," I told her. "I can understand what they're saying."

It turned out they did know a bit of English from grade school. Victor rotated his backpack to the front and pulled out a wooden box from the front pocket.

"Marijuana?" he asked and passed me a small glass pipe. Felipe pressed his fingers against his lips to contain his laughter.

"Did you learn that in school too?" I said with a smirk and handed the pipe to Celia. "You first."

The last time I'd smoked was with you, when your mother gave us a joint she had bought from her friend at the Y for her menopause. She wanted us to see if it was laced with opium.

"Mary tells me they ship it in cellophane boxes filled with Pine-Sol," she told us. "That's how they get it through security."

"That wouldn't work, Ma. The drug dogs can smell through Pine-Sol," you said and took the joint.

We didn't want to smoke on our stoop, worried the police might patrol on foot, so we leaned outside the bathroom window. I remember you were paranoid that the neighbors who worked in Admissions would report you to the school.

"Relax," I teased and blew a smoke cloud in your face.

We then got in bed and grazed each other's bodies with our fingertips—the outer edge of my foot, the bottom of my spine, the undersides of my breasts—giggling for hours.

The boys' weed wasn't very strong, but it was harsh. Celia took a puff and coughed uncontrollably, tears streaming down her face.

"Meu Deus," she said and passed it to me. I took a hit and held it inside until my lungs hurt.

"Rock and roll!" Felipe said, looking pleased. They rested their bikes one on top of the other and sat down next to us. Victor removed a digital camera from his backpack and clicked through pictures he'd taken around Paraty. He only took photographs of women, he told us, because they are much more beautiful than men. A bad pickup line, I thought, and yet there was something interesting about his portraits. Maybe it was the weed—the colors looked richer, the depth greater, edges sharpened. He showed us a photo of an old woman he saw on a bench with her husband, their limbs intertwined, a woven cape draped across her shoulders. He showed me another of a woman in a cobalt blue bikini, bending over to pick up a beach stone. He had a photo of his sister climbing a tree, her dangling hair framing her face as she looked down at the camera.

"Do you like them?" he asked, and Celia nodded.

He lifted the camera and pointed it at us.

"Posso?" he asked.

I hid my face behind my beach wrap. "No, no, no," I said, but he persisted, curving the camera around the wrap.

"Hey," I said and pushed it away.

He pointed the camera in my face, laughing.

"Really. Enough," I said and cupped my hand over the lens.

He heard the sternness in my tone and put the camera away. Felipe tried to make a bit of small talk about the weather, how it had been cloudy for days, but my interaction with Victor had soured the mood. They left shortly after, dragging their bicycles over the sand and into town. I felt a little embarrassed, but Celia seemed unfazed. She made a pillow with her wrap and lay back down on the sand.

"It's quiet again," she said and bent an arm over her eyes.

That's when the high really began to deepen. I could feel it vibrating in my eye sockets and fingernail beds and the tip of my tongue. I tilted my head back and let my cheeks droop.

"Do you feel that?" I turned to Celia but she didn't answer. She pulled her fingers through her hair and rolled onto her stomach. Maybe she couldn't hear me, I thought. Maybe I hadn't actually said anything.

"Celia?" I said again. "Celia?"

"Yes?"

"I couldn't let them take a picture of me. I left my husband to come here."

Again she didn't respond. I grabbed her arm.

"Please tell me you can hear me."

"Yes, I can hear you. You're being quite loud."

"What if he leaves me when I return?"

"Who? Your husband?"

"Yes."

"Are you afraid that he will?"

"I don't know. No, I don't think so."

"Linda," she said and rested her hand against my sternum, as if she could control my heart rate with the touch of her hand. "Relax. Lie down."

She pressed me to the ground, first to my elbows, and then fully against the sand. She kept her hand firm against my chest and nudged, ever so slightly, until I rested my eyes.

I must have fallen asleep, because when I woke, Celia was standing by the shoreline. I went to her.

"I'm ready for a swim," I said, and we dove in together.

After swimming we went to a bookstore café with tables set up on a cobblestone road and ate chocolate bonbons. We cracked the spines of unopened books—Clarice Lispector, Paulo Coelho, Paulo Freire—and marked the pages with our chocolate-stained fingers. We watched the sun expand across the buildings until the town turned a deep blue.

We decided to have dinner in our bathing suits rather than have to go back to the hostel. We ordered pizza and pitchers of beer at a small bar that opened onto the street. After the sun had fully set on the night sky, a crowd began to circle around a guitarist who played in the corner of the bar. He wore a large brimmed hat and sat on a wooden stool. The music started off softly, but became the central attraction once more people appeared. Celia took me by the hand and we joined in dance. Couples paired off and held each other by the fingertips, their legs swirling to the music. Their samba defied physics. Legs moved outward while hips pulled inward. The best dancers were admired and desired. Men cheered and clapped, women moved closer. Celia watched my flailing attempts to keep up.

"Don't worry," she said and pulled me toward her. "Look up. Smile."

Celia danced the best. I saw men watch her and try to move in, but she kept her attention on me, pushing my chin up when I stepped on her toes.

Then the guitarist played a song I had heard many times before. So had the crowd. If it were any other moment or any other place, they may have rolled their eyes—we heard this song in grocery stores and pharmacies, in car radios and restaurants. I even heard it at coffee shops and in elevators back home. But the familiarity was welcomed here. We all wanted to sing along. The guitarist tapped against the side of his guitar and sang the first lines to "Águas de Março" without any chords. Immediately the room erupted with joy.

"É pau, é pedra, é o fim do caminho."

It is wood, it is stone. It is the end of the road.

Then the guitar strings broke in and we danced. Celia took my hand and pressed me close to her, then twirled me away. We sang loudly, looking at each other straight in the eyes, the lyrics flowing from my smiling mouth in a way Portuguese never had before.

"É a vida, é o sol. É a noite, é a morte."

It is life, it is sun. It is night, it is death.

A young man who had been watching us from the side finally decided to step in. He wore an open green vest and a crystalline smile. He asked if he could dance with me. Celia obliged, finding it amusing, but stayed nearby. He danced at a respectful distance, perhaps too nervous to venture closer. Celia had stopped to have a sip of beer and clap for the guitarist. I had painted an image of us in my mind, catching fish off the shore, growing papaya and lime trees behind a thatched roof hut, with our own pier leading to the water, sleeping on the sand with Claudius curled at our feet. This already felt like our life. It is the waters of March ending the summer. For a moment, I had forgotten we had anything else.

The young man must have noticed that I hadn't paid him much attention. As soon as the song ended, he walked away without saying goodbye.

I went over to Celia.

"I'm tired. Let's go back home."

We shared a cigarette on our walk to the hostel. On the way, we saw Victor and Felipe riding their bicycles over the cobblestones.

"No photos!" Victor shouted.

"Cara de pau," Celia muttered, laughing, and we turned in to the hostel gates, the camping ground baked with the smells of soil and cut grass.

We went to bed in our separate bunks, clicked off the light, and let the lava lamp run. Then I heard Celia whisper: *Psst. I think I hear a noise.*

"Do you hear the noise?" she asked.

I told her no, I didn't hear a noise.

"I think the boys are outside. Felipe and Victor."

I paused to see if I could hear anything. I couldn't—only the chirr of crickets. I heard her rise from her bed and climb down the ladder.

"Could I sleep next to you?"

"Are you really afraid?" I asked and moved over to the edge of the mattress.

"I would prefer it, yes."

We both turned on our sides to fit, our arms unnaturally rigid. I could feel the awake energy between us, as if every hair on my body was pointing toward her. We lay like this for a few minutes before Celia spoke again.

"Are you asleep?" she asked.

"No."

She reached an arm around me, her armpit cupped on top of my shoulder, her hand limp against my stomach.

"I need to stretch," she said. "Is this okay?"

I nodded, but I feared she could sense my heart pounding through me. Her breath deepened, not with sleep but with strength, so that her chest pushed against my back and her exhales blew against the top of my head.

"Linda," I heard her whisper, then she inched her hand across my stomach, lifting up my gown. "Tell me what you're thinking."

Again I said nothing. I let her move her hand deeper and retreat, deeper and retreat, like a cat toying with a fish at the edge of a pond. I rolled over, her face and mine now touching, and kissed her chin—I couldn't make out where she was in the dark—then inched up and found her mouth.

I have a memory that I thought, No, I can't do this, and that I tried to get out. Dennis, I remember thinking. Where are you? But I also think it's possible that I invented this memory, as a defense, because in the moment I didn't stop. I started, I kept going, I allowed her, I got on top of her, I moved down her body, dragged her clothes down and up. I harnessed a sharp memory of my own pleasures. I remembered what I enjoy, what firmness I liked, what slowness, what my body needed, and I gave it to her. I ducked below her belly button and closed my eyes; it felt as though I could have been pressing my mouth against a warm, soft-bearded face. Except that Celia smelled like the expensive Italian soap she'd packed, and when I brushed my lips against hers, she kissed back with the press of her hips and the tips of her fingers against my forehead. Go on. I listened to her voice and followed. At first I was eager and nervous, tongue stiff and imprecise, but she held on to my shoulder and slowed me down. I kept pace, and she folded her hands behind her head. I realized that I already knew the way—her pleasure was mine and mine hers. The curves of our sensation mirrored each other, up, around, and down again. I too enjoyed the mystery when all sensations but touch and sound evaporated. She shook, grabbed on to my hair, and pulled me up, hugged me, kissed my mouth, and then let go.

I wasn't looking to turn away from you; I wasn't looking to replace you; I was searching for another version of myself. I found her in Celia—with her I was adventurous, I was new, I was the green of a leaf just peeking from the bulb. We pushed the sheets off the bed and pulled the fan up against our feet. She curled up and fell asleep pressed against the wall, and I stared, wide-eyed, at the springs underneath the top mattress.

Chapter Twenty-two

The fan stopped working. Somehow it had unplugged from the wall. I dragged myself down to the tiled floor and sucked in the coolness. Celia noticed that I had left the bed and reached her hand down for me, then shuffled off and lay on top of me.

"It's too hot, Celia."

She was heavy on my back. I couldn't move. She stuck her finger between my legs and dragged it through the moisture.

"Please, Celia," I said, and she got up.

"Do you mind if I shower first?" she asked and took the towel hung on the back of the chair.

It was the day we were meant to leave. I felt dense with confusion, like I couldn't remember the order of things: when we'd left, when I last saw you, how long Celia and I had been together. I couldn't measure what I'd done: Was it big enough to swallow our entire history, or so small it didn't even deserve an explanation?

I told myself that love isn't measured by how much we shared. What love is measured by, though, I couldn't answer.

The shower shut off. I got up from the floor and took my turn. She packed for me while I washed and dressed.

"Ready?" she asked. We slung our bags over our shoulders and left, her arm hugged around my waist.

At the bus station I noticed a pay phone across the street. I told Celia I needed to make a call while she bought our tickets. I wanted to see if you were home.

I twisted the cord around my fingers and read the devotions etched onto the side of the booth: R+J, N+O, L+T. It was Marta who finally picked up. I felt calmed to hear the sound of her voice.

"Aló?"

"Oi, Marta. It's Linda. Is Dennis home?"

"No. He's teaching." She paused. "Where are you?"

I saw Celia across the street. She had bought a red Popsicle and was leaning against a bus, dragging her tongue against the melting sides.

"I went to the beach for a few days. I'll be home in the evening."

"Okay. Should I tell Dennis?"

I told her yes, to let you know I'd called.

"Tá bom," she said, and for a moment the line went silent. "Are you with the woman you know?" she said. "Your Portuguese teacher."

I felt the sudden hollowness in my stomach.

"Yes," I said and wanted to apologize. "I'll be home soon."

I hung up and walked back across the street to Celia. She handed me her Popsicle, and I bit off the top.

"Did Dennis answer?" she asked. It was strange to hear your name come out of her mouth.

"No. It was Marta."

She smiled. "How is Marta?"

"She sounded worried, actually."

She handed me my ticket. "Let's get on the bus then."

The ride back to São Paulo was tense. Celia steered the conversation gradually. She told me about a play she hoped to bring to her theater, about how she needed actors, how she thought São Paulo might not be the right location.

"Will you talk to Rafael when you return?" I asked.

She shrugged. "Let's see how badly Karina destroyed the house."

Neither of us brought up what had happened the night before, until the bus pulled into the station and we said our goodbyes.

"Last night," I started to say, and I could feel the emotion rising inside me.

"Last night was for us and us only," she said and kissed me on the cheek.

The moment already felt so far away, and a part of me knew our relationship had reached a pivotal point, in the way a star becomes a supernova before it descends into a black hole.

Chapter Twenty-three

When I got home, you pretended you didn't hear me. I found you at the kitchen table thumbing through a textbook. I dropped my bag and you looked at me over your shoulder, then back down at the book.

"Oh," you said. "You're home."

For a moment I thought maybe you'd prefer not to talk about it, so I took my bag and tried to move past you. As I approached, I could feel the fury surrounding you, the kind that develops after days of silent rumination. You had replayed this very moment in your mind over and over again in a way that I hadn't. I looked through the door into the living room, through the window and at a tiny airplane passing through the sky.

"Yes," I said. "I'm home. I needed some time away to collect myself, but now I'm back."

You stood from the kitchen table, your lips pressed together so hard they turned white. For the first time in our marriage I thought you might hit me. You had reached the point right before the break of anger where you parroted my words back to me. "Home?" you repeated. "Some time?" I had nowhere to go, no argument to make. I braced myself for the blow. But you didn't get near me, which, at the time, felt worse.

"I'm going to the library," you said and picked up your books.

"Maybe we should talk."

"I have nothing to say to you. You should think about what you want to say to me."

The door slammed behind you.

Your reaction dipped into the pits of my anxiety. I thought about how you might return even more angered. By leaving I had threatened the viability of our marriage, and that terrified me. But this terror rubbed against the rejuvenation I felt from my brief stay in Paraty. Celia had pushed me toward my own body, toward my sense of physicality in the world. I had caught a glimmer of myself as someone who dug into her life with teeth and let the juice run down her chin. It was worth it to feel sticky afterward, but it wasn't worth it to lose you.

When I had resigned myself to being alone in the foggy cage of my thoughts, Marta suddenly appeared before me, in the living room, with her purse in her hand.

"Marta." I gripped my forehead and felt the beads of sweat soak into my fingers. "I didn't realize you were still here. I'm sorry you had to hear all that."

She explained that she was supposed to have left thirty minutes ago. She was running late. She had missed her bus.

"The next one is in two hours," she said.

The consequences of my decision extended beyond our relationship. Marta, too, would feel the impact. And although she was stronger than the mistakes I'd made, it wasn't fair that I had implicated her.

"Well," I said, sitting down in the kitchen chair. "I may not be the best company right now, but I'd really love for you to stay awhile."

I could see her ponder whether she should leave. She looked to her left down the hall, and then toward the back door. Then she looked at me.

"I can't stay long," she said. She put her purse on the table and sat in the chair next to me. It was such a relief that she agreed to stay, as though a vise had been released from my lungs.

Marta pulled out her fan and waved it at her face as she leaned her head against the kitchen wall. I could feel the breeze blow back to me, and I leaned forward to feel some more.

"How was Dennis?" I asked. "While I was gone."

She hummed and rocked her head back and forth. "Oh, he'll be all right."

"Do you really think so? Even if I've done something horrendous."

"Maybe you have. But that doesn't mean he won't forgive you. He's angry because he loves you very much."

This made me sad, not only for you but because Marta was being so compassionate.

"I'm sorry I brought you into this. If you want us to leave, I understand. We could go to a hotel. You shouldn't have to suffer because I turned up and caused this mess."

She laughed. "So you want to leave again? I know what it feels like to want to flee. But you cannot sacrifice your family for a taste of something new."

"I don't even think I want to flee anymore. I thought that was what I wanted, but I think more so I wanted to disappear. I wanted to become so unburdened that I would actually become invisible. And at the same time, I wanted desperately to be seen."

I slumped onto the table and rested my face on the cool surface. "I'm exhausted."

"You know, you remind me a little of my sister. She has

made some bad decisions in her life. But she's not a bad person. She hasn't learned enough about herself to see how she reflects out on the world."

As I studied my reflection in the table, Marta began to tell me about her sister, Felina, and how their relationship had evolved since they were children. I sat up and listened. I didn't interrupt her; I didn't ask questions. I just listened. She told me that at first she bore the burden of protecting Felina from the wildness of the world. Now they carry that burden together. Even then I understood that Marta was giving me something valuable by telling me about her life. At one point, in what felt like an enormous accomplishment, I got up to make us coffee and she let me make it for her. She did not stop speaking.

I want to pass on to you what Marta gave to me, her life's story, but I know it should be told in Marta's own words. My attempt to recollect what she said won't do the story justice. If I learned anything from our time in São Paulo, spent with Marta, with Celia, with you, it's that our collective experience should shape how history is remembered. I want my story to be remembered by how I evolved not only for myself, but for the important people in my life.

Chapter Twenty-four

MARTA'S STORY

My family claimed me by body parts from the day I was born. I had my father's toes, collarbones, and crooked hairline; my mother's spine, bowed lips, and soft belly. She's ours, they told our aunts, uncles, cousins, and neighbors, who had filled our creaky living room to witness my birth. They said they prayed on it before I was born, whose parts would be whose. And when I came out slick like a peeled plum boiled in sugar water, they saw in me the same life that they had seen for themselves.

☙

I grew up in Atibaia, a small country town an hour away from São Paulo, during the 1964 military coup d'état. My brother, sister, and I were all born where we were raised and where I still live today, in the house my father built in our neighborhood, Portão. Pai worked as a bricklayer, so he knew how to make a strong home, one that could stand against flooding and hailstorms. Other houses were strung together with found materials: plywood, black tarps, plastic piping, palm leaves. We were lucky, our mother told us nearly every day, because ours had sturdy walls and a roof, and a yard that kept a chicken coop, a beehive, and a brown-and-black mule named Beto.

I still have a drawing Mãe made of our house when we were children. Its thick shades of brown and green, a dirt road out front with dusty dogs wading in a dry basin. Our neighbors, many Tupi and African like us, tilled soil, picked strawberries, sold roses out of a metal pushcart in town. These were the people we danced next to in the congada line—our community, our church family. Today, though, my neighborhood is a faint reflection of what it used to be. I see houses with satellite dishes and swimming pools. Where a person once stood in the field, a machine now rumbles.

❧

My sister and I slept in the bedroom, my brother in the living room, and my parents in a shed in the back. Once a month, Pai would take Beto into town to get drinking water and big burlap bags of rice and beans that he slung across Beto's hind legs and hobbled up the steep roads. Pai liked these trips because he liked to be alone, even when he was around people. I saw myself in him. A snail rolled into a shell. He had deep, dark skin, the kind you fall into, and that was mine too. The other side of the moon kind. A crystal lake at dusk kind. My mother's complexion turned the world cross-eyed. She looked browner than the Japanese farmers who lived in the strawberry fields, but lighter than Pai and me, and darker than Felina and Henrique. Depending on the angle of the sun, she could be any number of constellations. Her mother called her light, her sister called her dark, the rest called her parda, a color in between.

❧

Before I was born into consciousness, before I heard the boys at school call me preta, pretinha, little black girl, Mãe would hold me in her arms, arms that were not mine but hers, and point to the parts we shared. Hair, heart, hunger. I took these parts with me and wore them around. People liked to guess what my mother was. One woman in town—a stranger wearing a sunbonnet and grass-woven slippers—even asked if she was half Japanese. This made me laugh. Mãe covered my face, told me to stop, but all I could do was laugh. I had many different laughs. Confused, nervous, tickled, unsure. I couldn't stop laughing, so my mother dragged me out of the store by my wrist, down the road, through the church doors, and into salvation.

&

The boys who called me pretinha played soccer on the red-dirt field rimmed with palm trees. I walked by there every day on my way home from school. My aunt had called me pretinha since the day Felina was born, because of the three of us, I was the dark one. The word had a softness when she said it to me as a child, minha pretinha, cuddling her fingers under my chin. But it grew edges as I got older and the schoolboys began to shout it at me from a distance. It was as though each time I heard the word, pretinha, I swallowed a little stone, until eventually those stones filled my body and I had no room for any more. They took it, the boys did, the part I shared with my father, our velvet, the only part that I shared with him that no one else did, not Mãe, not Felina, not Henrique. I felt the final shrill inside me, the scratch on my gut, pretinha, pretinha, pretinha, when they called to me in unison from the middle of the field.

My name is Marta, I yelled to them. You assholes!

A tall boy with a purple thread tied into his hair pushed the soccer ball into my stomach and asked me who gave me my pau, the dick between my legs. He ran away chanting: pretinha, pretinha, pretinha. When I got home, I told my aunt never to call me that again.

&

My mother cleaned houses and my father laid bricks. That's how they made their money. The same way I make my money now: with sweat and surrender. Mãe cooked a week's worth of rice and beans in deep steel pots, served with our hen eggs and collard greens from the garden. We all knew how to ration, how much to spoon into the bowl, how to train our bellies to want less. My father taught me how to slaughter a chicken, pluck its feathers, retrieve the liver and heart (my mother's favorite parts), and butcher it from neck to tail. My mother taught me how to divide money—one coffee can in a hole under the mattress. A jar in the back of the refrigerator. An envelope in her dress pocket for bills and food. She taught me how to sew a broken button together, to rub the dark streaks out of a pan, how to water a garden using dishwater. My brother taught me how to treat a cough with chamomile tea, small cuts with lamb's ears leaves, and to put mint under my pillow for good dreams.

&

My sister, Felina, taught me how to love. She was born in our living room, fell into our aunt's hands, three years after me. She was a perfect blend of my mother and my father, and I remember how frustrated I felt not being able to claim her by parts like my parents had claimed me. Everything she had could be shared. Her body was strong and slender, her face sweet and assured. She was caramel and soft and dark and light and safe and beautiful. I held her in my arms and called her my baby.

&

On dry days, when rain hadn't washed away the trails, my father
would take me and my sister on the back of the mule to the top
of Pedra Grande mountain. Atibaia was built at the foot of
Pedra Grande, a holy rock that protected the town like a for-
tress. We would lie on the sun-warmed stone slabs at the peak
and watch the low clouds and wide sky and the small specks of
São Paulo's city line on the horizon. Pai would pack a canteen
of hot water and his chimarrão gourd. He pressed the wet,
green mate against the side of the gourd and took the first, bit-
ter sip, then passed the metal straw to me. I liked chimarrão
with honey, but my father drank mate like a vaqueiro, and I was
his vaqueira. Only Mãe let me have it sweet.

⚘

I tell this story now, at forty-five years old, wondering for the
first time what it truly means to die. For my father, thirty years
after I was born, his heart gave up, and then the rest of him followed. For my mother it's been her kidneys, then hips, but she
hasn't gone yet. If I were to guess, of all my parts, I would say my
breasts would betray me first. My arms have always been loyal. I
have a strong spine. My lungs, heart, and stomach have worked
tirelessly for many years, even when I wasn't the best to them. But
my breasts are the Gemini sisters of my being—at once charming
and aloof, confidantes one moment, strangers the next.

   This is the story of my breasts:

- I taped them down when they got too big.
- I ran my fingers across the light stretch marks that wove into
  my skin.
- I held them up, cupped in my hands, when gravity pulled,
  sore and tired and needing a lift.
- I dreamt about surgeries to make them smaller; an insertion
  in the side to remove the excess, the weight, the part that
  draws attention.

■ Now they are a part of me just as much as any part. That is to
say, they are me.

❧

By the time she was five I could already see the change in Felina.
I could see the way strangers looked at her. The same woman
who'd asked if my mother was half Japanese stopped us to say
how enchanting Felina was. She took her cheeks into her palms
and told her that she was a wonder of Venus. I once asked my father if Felina was prettier than me. And he said, yes, she is, but
beauty is a curse. He had given me so much of his body, everything that was given to him. For many years, into adulthood, I
wished that I could take some of that pretty from her. I wanted
to save her from the hurt that her beauty would become.

❧

I spent most of the year 1967 waiting by our window. The
Armed Forces had won—we were officially under military rule.
I was eight, my sister was five, and my brother was twelve. When
I came home from school and my parents were still at work, I
would watch the birds bathing in dust pools outside the window, longing for the moment my mother would walk through
the door. My brother looked after us in the afternoon before
leaving to play soccer, then a neighbor would come to make
sure we hadn't fallen or burned ourselves or swallowed anything whole. Every day I begged my mother to take me to work.
I didn't like one of the neighbors who came to watch us. I had
heard him use a belt on his own children, through the wooden
fence dividing our backyards. Thwaps and cries. But every day
was the same: my mother would push my sobbing face from her
calf, and I would go to the window, waiting, and waiting.

❧

When I think back on those days, my best memories are from when everyone was together at home. Mãe, Pai, Henrique, Felina, and me. Mãe liked to poke fun at Pai just to make us laugh, and he took it just to keep us laughing. She once told him she wanted to eat the dirt under his cracked nails until they were clean. Pai was self-conscious about his permanently stained hands, blackened from decades of bricklaying. He would hide his hands in his pockets when we went to church. Mãe pretended to gobble his fingers. We laughed in horror. He told her she had mean teeth, and kissed her smile.

When I think of Mãe, I see her sitting on a stack of pillows and playing the guitar, wearing one of her hand-stitched floral dresses. I stuck my face under her skirt once and saw the shock of black hair, two angular breasts. She liked to be nude so that the breeze would blow against her, she said. She would let me billow the hem of her dress so that it rippled like waves.

❦

One day, Mãe came home early from work. This had never happened before, so when I saw her walking by the fence and across our backyard, half her body slumped over, one hand covering her mouth, I ran from the window to her and wrapped my arms around her legs. She had contracted a parasite (we later learned it was tapeworm) and walked home from work, a two-hour journey by foot, in the midday sun, stopping occasionally to vomit on the side of the road. Cars tried to stop and offer her a ride, but she waved them off, afraid she might soil their upholstery. I felt overwhelmed to see her. I couldn't stop squealing. She told me to be quiet, that her head hurt. Her skin was tense and moist. She splashed cold water from the kitchen sink onto her neck and underneath her armpits.

Where is your sister? she asked, wiping her mouth with the hem of her dress.

I pointed to the bedroom door, which was closed, something my mother didn't allow. She made the face she makes when she says she isn't in the mood, and opened the door.

ꙮ

When she screamed, I assumed it was because she was angry with Felina for sneaking our great-grandmother's teacups into the bedroom to play with her doll. But then she kept scream-ing, and I saw the neighbor's shadow leap out of the window, run through the yard and over his fence. I stood in the door-frame to see what had happened. My mother had Felina clutched in her arms, and Felina looked like she had been soak-ing in the tub for too long, like the water had gone cold and washed all the color away.

ꙮ

After my mother found the neighbor in my sister's room, she began bringing us to work. She was a maid in a gated commu-nity at the bottom of Pedra Grande. On the days we had school, we had to take a bus to the gate and wait for her to get us. My sister and I would lie in the grass and watch hang gliders propel off the side of the cliff, over the big, white houses with swim-ming pools, over the trees with red flowers the size of my face, and land somewhere between our house and theirs.

But when we crossed to the other side of the gate, we also crossed into a different side of Mãe. She was quiet in these houses. She told us to stay in the maid's closet and to be quiet too, quiet like work-mom is quiet, that the quieter we were the shorter it would be. We would sit in there for hours, sometimes ten hours at a time, and watch American Westerns on the small black-and-white TV. I began to learn English this way, through John Wayne and Clint Eastwood. I was very good at it. The sen-tences stuck easily in my mind. At one house I could hear the dona's daughter taking English lessons in the kitchen. I would turn down the television and listen, correcting her mistakes in my head.

❧

Felina and I invented a new game we called city girls. We would prop our mattress up on its side and pretend it was a giant building, a skyscraper, then circle around it like we were going to our city jobs. We invented the game from what we had seen at the houses where Mãe worked—pictures on the wall, hints of conversations. We had no idea what happened in the city, but we pledged to each other that we would go there someday. We would put on Mãe's floral dresses so that they dragged on the ground, as if they were long, elegant gowns, and bump into each other in our hurry to and from our jobs in the giant mattress.

Excuse me, where is your maid! Felina said to me.

I don't need one! I said. My house is always clean!

❧

We were sitting in an unused sauna while my mother cleaned the house's pool. I asked my sister, What did he do to you, while I was waiting by the window? She drew a circle around her body using a stick from the garden and dropped to the floor. I knelt next to her and lifted her head from the wooden floorboards. She kept her eyes staring straight ahead, like we did when we played dead, her neck limp, until I told her she could come alive now.

You'll never play alone again, Felina. I'm here, my sister.

She nodded, shut her eyelids, and curled her body into my lap.

❧

I saw my parents, late one night, sitting at the kitchen table. The light from the overhead lamp cast an orange glow on my mother's cheekbones, my father's face rested in his hands.

What did you see? he asked her. Tell me what you saw.

I didn't see. I felt it. I smelled it. I am her mother.

I know, querida, he kept saying, again and again, his face sinking deeper into itself. I will talk to him.

🌿

After we started going to work with Mãe, I only ever saw the neighbor after the sun had set, when he would sit in the back of his house to smoke a pipe alone. I tiptoed to the fence that divided us and listened to the tobacco crackle as he took a long pull, followed by one distinct, guttural cough. I imagined touching the pipe bowl with the tip of my fingers, the wood hot against my skin, and pushing, pushing, pushing it into his mouth. No, he'd try to say, his eyes gasping for air. The burning tobacco emptied onto his tongue, and with each inhale, a plume of smoke and embers buried into his lungs. He was rendered to ash, a gray heap beneath this story.

🌿

And then, as if the wind blew, he vanished. I listened for the sounds of his children next door, the cries from the belt, the stench of tobacco at night. But he was gone.

The soldiers took him, I told Felina. They shoved him into the back of a camouflaged truck. His feet were dangling out the back window. They drove him to the jungle and fed him to piranhas.

How do you know? she asked. Did you see it?

I felt it, I told her. I smelled his wet tobacco stench drifting down the road.

🌿

Even now my mind plays tricks on me, wonders if it could have happened at all. I was sitting by the window the entire time. How did I not hear? How did I not feel it? On bad days I punish myself. On better days I pray to God and ask for forgiveness. On good days I say, You were a child too, Marta. You were a child too.

&

So how did I become a maid? It's a question I asked myself for years, until I realized that the question had flattened my sense of being, that the question bore the weight of centuries, and even fate didn't have the courage to answer to it. Why should I?

The truth is, my parents had to choose. My brother, Henrique, the oldest, was the only one who could finish high school. He would leave the house at 5:00 A.M. and walk to a better school that was closer to town. I never made it through the eighth grade. I had to stay home, look after the house, take care of my sister, work. We had all gone to school together, Felina, Henrique, and I, in the same building where we went to church, a house with the walls removed from the inside. Dona Sadi was our teacher. She taught ages seven through fifteen, sometimes at the same time, and her husband was a bricklayer like our father. After the military took over, the government stopped sending money to schools like ours. The school building had leaks in the roof, so if it rained, we all had to sit on one side of the classroom. We didn't have pencils or paper or enough books for everyone in class. Sometimes Dona Sadi would read aloud passages to us and we would have to listen, then repeat back what she said. This is why many of us still could not read by the time we left school—we never got to see the words on the page.

&

On my fourteenth birthday, my uncle came to our house with a bundle of books that he'd found in town. A wealthy family was moving, he said, and left half their life on the street for others to take. There were cookbooks and a dictionary and an old almanac. Felina wasn't interested in the slightest, and Henrique already got books in school, so I had my pick. He even brought a book written in English, *Treasure Island*, that had English notes scribbled in the margins. I used these books to practice reading even after I had to leave school to help my parents. Literature became my secret retreat. I shared everything with my brother and sister, but these books were my own. I kept them under my bed and read them when no one was around. I even tried to pronounce the words in the English book until my mouth felt worn, like I had to exercise to get the sounds out.

❧

Felina and I moved out of our parents' home when she got pregnant. It was 1977—she was fifteen and I was eighteen. Our family and neighbors made up a story that we had been swept away by charming men. They all pretended like it was true, feigned admiration, jealousy even, and my mother went along with the fable. She didn't want to admit that her youngest was having a child out of wedlock, or else she'd blame herself for not keeping a closer watch.

❧

The baby's father lived in São Paulo. His name was Luis, and he was ten years older than Felina. To mask his insecurity over their difference in age, he professed that it was just a number, that Felina was mature for her age, that inside Felina's young body lived a very old soul, that he had met women three times her age who understood half as much about the world as she did. This may have been true, but he was wrong. Felina was a child. And yet, still, if Luis hadn't impregnated my sister, I might have felt bad for him. He was desperately in love with her and believed that they were destined for each other, that they might spend the rest of their lives together. Luis himself looked much younger than he actually was. He had round, supple cheeks that could not grow hair, and reminded me of a hairless rabbit with a mouth full of grass. I watched the way he watched Felina. I could see the stories he told himself about her.

- Felina, the princess in a high turret, birds twitching on her shoulders, frogs leaping at her feet
- Felina, the chocolate torte his mother made for him when he was a child
- Felina, a cat that crept in shadows, balanced on windowsills a hundred feet in the air, her spine contorting and twisting to better fit tricky angles
- Felina, the lonely prisoner, and Luis, a chink in the wall

A few days after she told our mother, I found Felina soaking in the bathtub, something she hardly ever did. Only her breasts, face, and hands peaked from the surface; the rest of her body looked dark underwater, dressed in tiny bubbles that clung to her edges.

I asked her, Have you talked to Pai?

Our father had all but disappeared from the house since the news broke.

He's spending more time on Pedra Grande, she said.

Yes. He takes a bottle with him.

I don't expect him to understand, she said, and sank her face into the water. I held on to her hand.

It will be different when the baby is here.

❧

Felina specifically requested that I go and live with them in São Paulo. She told Luis she needed my help through the pregnancy—that there were things happening with her body that he wouldn't understand. Felina had dealt with terrible sickness, vomiting day and night. She was skinny in her face, arms, and legs, but with a bulbous stomach, like a black widow spider. Through this sickness she grew intolerant of most people, and Luis was at the center of this intolerance. So he obliged, and we left my parents, my brother, our chickens and bees. We left Atibaia and moved to the city with Luis.

Luis's home was a gap in space between the other places he had to go. The walls were bare but for a calendar, three years old, hung in the living room. He had a small futon, where I would sleep, and a bedroom with a mattress and a mirror propped on the floor. There weren't enough cups for each of us to have a drink at the same time, so when we arrived Luis opened a beer from the fridge and poured a little into two glasses, then took the rest himself.

I shouldn't drink, Felina told me, and gave me her glass.

⚜

My mother begged for me to keep watch over Felina in São Paulo. Though I was just eighteen years old myself, teenage girls were being kidnapped off the streets, shoved into vans, and held for ransom or sold into slavery. In my mother's words, they would see her and the baby as a two-for-one deal. So I made sure Felina only left Luis's apartment when I left the apartment, and I only left the apartment to go to and from my job as a maid at several homes in Moema.

⚜

We had heard stories about rich people who wasted water in the shower so that we, the poor people, couldn't have any. When I thought about these water wasters, I pictured the white couple who owned the jewelry store in town in Atibaia. I didn't know what real rich was until I began to clean houses in São Paulo. My family was poor, but we weren't as poor as the farmers in the field houses. I grew up in a neighborhood where everyone worked outside—we all had cracked skin and callused palms. Even the store owners in town had to go outside to lift a box once in a while. I didn't know how precious hands could be, like the underside of a white rose petal, until I met São Paulo professors. I once saw a dona cut her finger while flipping a newspaper page; a single drop of red blood dotted the real estate section.

ॐ

Luis had a few different jobs—as an usher at a downtown movie theater, as a gas station attendant, as a weed dealer at the University of São Paulo. Because of his boyish face, he could easily slip in and out of the campus without provoking other dealers or police officers, or police officer drug dealers, who ran the neighborhood. In fact, the day Luis and Felina met he was hustling in Atibaia, in front of the ice cream store on the square. Felina was eating a coconut ice cream cone with friends after church, when Luis approached her and gave her a hand-rolled joint with a red heart drawn in washable marker on the side. He was visiting his aunt, he told her. They walked behind a plywood wall at a nearby construction site and finished her ice cream, smoked the joint. Felina knew even then that she would be bored by him, but she was fifteen and fascinated by the idea of independence, by the idea of an escape from our parents' farm, by an escape to São Paulo. Motherhood was her ticket out. She didn't understand that youth was the best kind of freedom, and she had squandered it for a bit of semen and pot and an admiring eye.

❦

Her romance with Luis and São Paulo was short-lived. Felina fled in the middle of the night, when she was seven months pregnant. She stole just enough money from Luis to pay for the bus fare back to Atibaia. She left without telling me. Luis and I woke up and found her note taped to the refrigerator.

> *Luis,*
>   *Visit us in Atibaia, always, whenever you need, but I do not want to raise her in São Paulo. I want her to run barefoot in the mountains.*

> *My dear Marta,*
> *I will see you at home.*
>   *Kisses,*
>   *Felina*

Luis dug his teeth into his bottom lip and shrieked from the inside of his mouth. Then he pounded his forehead against the refrigerator door, once, and then again, and again. I stood frozen, pretending to be invisible, sure that if I remained still he might forget that I had been there at all. But then he shriveled, decayed, and cried heaving sobs. I wet a dishrag and draped it across his forehead, then sat with him on the floor, my hand on his back, wondering if Felina had made it to Atibaia safely, if she was with my parents, and what they thought about her return. We sat for what must have been an hour, maybe longer, until the phone rang. It was my mother. She had used the neighbor's phone to call Luis's.

Where is Felina?

She's not with you?

That is exactly where she is. And you let her leave the apartment without you?

Mãe—she didn't tell me she was leaving. She left in the middle of the night.

And you didn't wake? How could you not have woken? Does Luis live in a castle?

I heard something, but I thought maybe she was going to the bathroom. I didn't think she would leave for good!

You need to keep an eye on your sister.

Is she safe?

Yes. She is eating a banana in the living room.

&

I stayed with Luis in São Paulo until Felina's baby was born. There were several reasons for this, the biggest one being that I did not want to go back to the farm. Since I had started making more money, enough to give half to my parents and keep half for myself, I could see a future outside of Atibaia. I could see a future in São Paulo. I had been cleaning apartments for the university for about three months by the time Felina left. I liked working for the professors. They too hoarded books in unusual places—underneath their beds, on the kitchen table, beside the toilet, on the windowsill. I liked to dust and replace them in their specially organized disorder, carefully fanning them in wobbly stacks. Sometimes I would open up the pages and search for graphs, just to admire the scattered dots that, to me, looked like birds taking flight. It was all new, and now, in a few short months, everything from my life before appeared worn in my memory; a bare tree covered in caterpillar webs.

&

It took me weeks to call Felina after she left. She wouldn't call me for fear that Luis would answer, so that gave me space to approach her on my own. I was upset that she left without telling me. But that anger broke like a fever in the night, and more than ever I missed my sister.

I called the neighbors and asked if they could get Felina for me. I gave them the number to call me back, then waited. I pictured Felina, pregnant, pulling herself off the rocking chair my father built and dragging her bare feet across the grass.

Olá? she said as soon as she heard the receiver pick up.

Felina.

Why haven't you called me?

You left without warning.

You left me every day when I was in São Paulo.

I didn't leave you. I was working.

I was alone in that apartment, day in and day out, with nothing but my thoughts. I could have died from boredom.

What did you want me to do? Not go to work?

That's why I left. Now you can go to your job without worrying about me.

I came to São Paulo for you.

And you stayed for?

My job, filha.

I heard her wince, like the baby had pressed against her.

I don't want to fight, she said. Will you be back to see the baby?

I'll come back to Atibaia when the baby is born.

I heard her breath blow into the phone.

I miss you, Marta. I hope the baby comes soon.

࿇

None of the professors I worked for knew anything about Atibaia. Often I would have to point to the town on a map to prove that it was real. Because they hadn't heard of Atibaia, they also hadn't heard of me or my family or the people I grew up with. When they inevitably asked the question What was it like to grow up in Atibaia? I somehow found it easier to invent an answer rather than explain the truth.

I told them that I was an only child of two schoolteachers. I said that my parents had homeschooled me until I was eighteen years old. It made the professors feel comfortable, relieved even, that their maid wasn't another poor black girl, and this gave me relief too. Each professor told the Provost that I was a top-notch maid: intelligent, forthright, discerning. I soon became one of their most in-demand employees. Like my mother, I have learned when it's important to stay quiet, and when I can play guitar and sing.

❧

I sometimes wonder, even still, how my life would be different if I had stayed in São Paulo instead of going back to Atibaia to help Felina. Would I have met a man myself? A rich, widowed professor who owned one of the apartments I cleaned? Would I have worked my way up the university hierarchy, a maid turned lecturer? Would I have saved enough money to buy my own apartment and my own car and start my own business?

In reality, I don't think my life would have been much different than it is now. Maybe I would have married a man and spent my life cleaning the house for him. I can't choose how far I want my destiny to stretch, as a girl from Atibaia, parts made from a black bricklayer and a maid. My years were stitched together long before my parents had begun to pray for something different, before the thread could come undone. I am happy with the life I have sewn.

❧

This is how I weave happiness into my days:

- I shell shrimp to make stock. I like to pull the translucent casing off of the white flesh and watch it boil.
- I listen to my nephew Mateus sing "The Itsy-Bitsy Spider" in English.
- I read the poetry books Henrique brings me, and I drink the wine he brings too.
- I watch my mother sit in the first pew at church, tapping her foot to the sound of the organ chords.
- I sit on the kitchen floor with Felina, after the children have gone to bed, and we read each other's horoscopes. We chase imagined worlds together from the protection of our home.

The day Felina gave birth to her first child, Sebastian (a baby boy, contrary to what she'd dreamt), no one from the neighborhood came to witness. This was at Felina's request. She only wanted me, Mãe, Pai, Henrique, and our aunt present. Not even Luis came—he claimed it would be too painful—but Felina didn't even seem to notice.

She gave birth to Sebastian in the same living room where she and Henrique and I were born. My aunt took Felina's hands and guided them to Sebastian's body so that she could pull him into the world herself. She placed him on her chest, and he cried and cried and didn't stop crying until he fell asleep.

He has your forehead. And he's loud like you, my mother said.

He is strong like you too, I said.

I don't know, Felina said, wiping his eyes and ears with a warm, soaked dish towel. I think this child is new. I think he knows more about himself than I could ever tell him.

Chapter Twenty-five

You would hardly look at me after I returned home from Paraty, let alone speak to me. Instead, you took your anger out on the apartment. You left dirty plates next to the mattress where you now ate dinner; you spat toothpaste into the kitchen sink and allowed it to crust; you ate in the middle of the night and left sticky surfaces to attract ants and flies.

If there was a silver lining, it was that my relationship with Marta had taken flight ever since we spent those hours together, when she told me about her childhood in Atibaia. Though she and I understood the paradox in your aggression—that it was, in this sense, my fault—she knew that I was sorry and that I wanted to make it right. She didn't blame me, she forgave me, and for that I was eternally grateful. We became unlikely allies during your time of anger, braving the passing storm together. One day I found her scraping a pan with eggs that you burnt. I apologized.

"Oh god," I said. "Let me."

"Don't worry," she said, removing globs of egg from the drain. "He spilled something in the bathroom that I'll let you handle."

Her humor and ease about the situation made everything a bit easier.

You began to come home from school earlier. You stopped offering office hours. You wrote and researched at home. Sometimes you even returned home for lunch and then left briefly for your afternoon lecture and returned again. You were afraid that I was going to leave you again, and I worried that if I left the apartment at all you'd explode, accuse me of abandoning you, and then wreck our home even more. So I stayed near you, even if we didn't interact. The two of us, and Marta.

Celia didn't call. I began to assume that I had done something wrong. Maybe it had been a mistake to sleep with her—maybe I had disintegrated a necessary distinction between friend and lover. I had been driven by a desire to know her body better than I knew my own body, to envelop myself in her sensuality, and though that desire felt complete, finished, I missed my friend. Her absence built inside the clock, the hands ticking slower and slower, hours clogged with minutes, until a week passed and I couldn't wait any longer. I tried to call her. The phone rang. She didn't answer. Another week passed. My thoughts evolved like the phases of the moon—sometimes whole, sometimes just a sliver, sometimes gone all together. I concocted situations: Maybe someone had died. Maybe she had left unexpectedly for work. This possibility only provided momentary relief until I unraveled it. Of course someone hadn't died! How could it ever be so simple? I had to invent another horrific scenario to yield any comfort.

The truth is, I couldn't divide my experiences into the nows, the forgottens, and the forevers, the way that Celia did. The past and the future entered and exited my thoughts like two rivers running against each other. This difference allowed Celia to keep me in her past, and made it impossible for me to remove her from my future.

One day Marta decided to cook a big lunch so we'd have to eat at the kitchen table together. She didn't say so, but I knew that was her plan.

I sat down against the wall, expecting you to sit across from me, but you sat beside me (probably so that you didn't have to look at me) as though we were two judges on a panel, watching Marta perform in the kitchen. You offered her suggestions and praise—Not so much salt for me, Marta; Linda put the colander in the upper cabinet; I like your shoes, Marta. Did you buy them in São Paulo?

She put plates of chicken Milanese in front of us.

"Nice that you are eating lunch together," she said and smiled at me, then tried to retreat into the laundry room. You reached out your hand, desperately, and asked her to stay.

"Please. Eat with us!"

She didn't verbalize her hesitation, just inched toward the laundry room.

"Marta," you said again and caught her arm. "I insist."

So she made herself a small plate and sat at the table across from us.

She ate in a hurry, finishing half her food before you were finished talking about your latest research on the American whaling industry in the eighteenth century. You broke down an entire whale from head to tail at the kitchen table: how they used the oil from blubber to burn lanterns, the bones for scrimshaw, the whale's digestive infections for perfume and soap. I soon lost my appetite. When you finally stopped speaking to try a bite of food, Marta asked if you were on a break from school.

"No," you responded. "Why?"

"You've been home more."

You scoffed. "Ask Linda."

I didn't answer.

"It's because *she* needs company." You pointed your thumb at me.

"That's not true," I said.

Marta placed her utensils on the empty plate and edged out her chair.

"Getting more food?" you asked. "You should have some more."

"I need to finish cleaning," she said. "My sister will be here soon."

"Don't worry about the apartment," you said. "We can live with a little dust on the shelves—"

"Come on, Dennis," I interrupted. "Let her go."

"So now everyone wants to leave!" you said and pushed out your chair. I thought you might cry.

"It's okay," Marta said. "I'll stay awhile longer."

She rested her elbows on the table and cradled her chin in her palms. You shoveled the chicken into your mouth, not even bothering to taste it. I tried to make eye contact with Marta to show that I didn't mean to trap her, but she kept her gaze on a grain of rice that she pushed around with her fork.

Your mood was sporadic and intense. You began to mutter on about how you never thought, growing up in Brookline, that you'd one day be in South America, married, with a doctorate, teaching at a university. You'd never thought of yourself as an intelligent person; your mother often told you, in her pin-striped aprons, that you were persistent but not an academic, and that school had been for you a miserable, taunting experience until the seventh grade, when you grew taller and leaner, joined a pickup basketball team at a court in Allston, and discovered Cervantes; that you learned to love history and literature from your grandfather, who immigrated to New Bedford from Portugal and worked in an oil refinery; he wasn't intelligent but he was cunning, and he knew a lot about the whaling industry. Which reminded you, you interrupted yourself abruptly, that you had more research to do. You left the kitchen and shut yourself in the bedroom.

Marta and I looked at each other. We cleared the dishes, then I went to find you.

You, cross-legged on the bed with your glasses on, papers strewn as though you'd tossed them into the air. When I entered you immediately barked, "I'm concentrating, Linda. Can you stay in the living room?"

We still slept in the same bed, but there was no touching. I could feel the firmness of your body from a foot away, turned toward the wall, the covers wrapped tight around you. It made it difficult to fall asleep. I would roll to my side and the sheets would straighten with tension. You weren't going to let me have an inch of slack. What did you think of me during these weeks? Did you pity my boring life, or did you envy the fact that I had no obligations? You spent most of your time facedown in books, glancing up occasionally to observe me walking from one room to the next, feigning activity.

On the worst days I thought about divorce. Maybe I should wait out our time in São Paulo, patiently, I thought, and then find a lawyer as soon as we returned to the United States. In my mind I divided our belongings: I'd keep my mother's mirror and the bed frame we got as a wedding gift, my art supplies, and the bread maker. You could have everything else.

A phone call from Melinda finally broke the spell. She specifically asked for me when you answered, and so you had to ask me what she wanted after we hung up. Their friend Hugo was having a Christmas party at an art gallery in her neighborhood and we were invited. You told me that I needed to act presentable, that we couldn't bicker like this in front of them, so even though you weren't actually happy with me, pretending was better than nothing.

Chapter Twenty-six

Hugo owned the gallery. He was an Australian whom Melinda and Eduardo had met twenty years ago, she told us, when he was still trying to break new ground as a painter, before he realized that the money wasn't in painting, it was in dealing. Hugo was no longer a starving artist—his belly strained the opal buttons on his collared shirt. I couldn't help but watch it, like a soft-boiled egg being pressed with the side of a fork. He gave us a tour of the gallery the night of the party, one hand stretched out to a canvas, the other reaching for a skewered piece of filet mignon on a serving tray.

His assistants had decorated the gallery ceiling in white lights and miniature disco balls that glimmered reflections off the paintings and sculptures. The servers wore red velvet dresses and passed effervescent cocktails with curly lemon peels snaked up the inside. The guests were a mixed group—some ragtag academics huddled in circles discussing the merit of modern art, while others were polished financiers contemplating pricing and size. What brought everyone together to the event, though, and what made this particular party special, Hugo explained, was a red balloon bunny statue, about the size of a jug of milk, propped on a pedestal in the center of the room. It was being auctioned off for two million dollars.

"It's on loan to us," Hugo explained. "I have a friend who knows the artist. He has a vested interest in promoting the gallery"—he winked—"so we're able to have it for the week."

You listened but you didn't react. Usually this was the kind of conversation that you thrived on, even if you thought it was ridiculous. Instead you held on to my hand or elbow or waist, asking me several times, to the side, if you had any food in your teeth. Our quartet bobbed through the crowd together—occasionally a friend of Eduardo's would come over to say hi, but mostly Eduardo and Melinda were glued to us, wanting to know our opinions of the art, asking us to guess prices, pointing to guests and whispering everything they knew about them.

Eventually Melinda pulled me away to go with her to the bathroom. I wondered if she was going to ask me about my disappearance, but she didn't. While we were washing our hands she told me that she and Eduardo had had a quarrel earlier in the evening over her mother's heirloom rug. He had sold it without telling her. She paused to adjust the brooch that she had fastened to her bun and I could see her eyes turn glossy with tears. I rubbed the top of her back to console her, but she patted her cheeks and said she was fine. She turned away, swung open the bathroom door to return to the party, and another couple quickly snatched her attention. I wandered off to find more champagne.

I noticed the long, thin reach of a server as she picked up an empty glass from a viewing bench. She glided between the backs of partygoers engaged in conversation, a bottle of Perrier-Jouët in hand, looking for a flute to fill. Her thin hair shook behind her, hips leading the rest of her body, legs crossed one slightly in front of the other. If it weren't for the red velvet uniform, I would have assumed she was a guest who knew Hugo well enough that he had given her her own champagne bottle.

I held out my empty glass. She came by and tipped the bottle without looking at my face. Instantly I recognized her. It was Simone, Celia's friend from the theater.

"You know me?" I said in my best Portuguese. "I know you?"

"Pardon?" She topped off the bubbles so that they floated slightly above the rim, then settled back down.

"My name is Linda. The friend of Celia."

Her face expanded.

"Ah! Yes. Linda." She nodded. "Of course."

"How are you?"

"I'm well. How are you?"

"I'm well."

We paused, looking vacantly in opposite directions. I didn't have enough words to continue politely, so I went ahead and asked her.

"How is Celia?"

"Celia?" Her eyes searched behind me, as if Celia might be at the party. "You don't know? She left São Paulo. She ran away with Rafael."

"Rafael?"

Though I sounded surprised, this suspicion had been living inside me for weeks. Where else would she go? She had loved him. She told me she loved him.

"Rafael and Celia," I said and clutched my hands together to express their closeness, as lovers, as paramours.

"Yes," she said. "They left together as lovers." She leaned in closer to my ear. "I heard they fled in the middle of the night without telling Karina. Rafael packed two suitcases and paid their neighbor to keep them in his apartment. Karina was asleep in their bed when they snuck away."

"And what happened to her?"

Simone smiled. Karina was devastated, of course. She had lost her partner, her love, the man who hoisted her in the iron cage. "But Karina is a survivor. She knows how to create in the midst of devastation. Her art is more reflective than ever."

Years later I learned what Celia and Rafael had run off to do, because the film they made together came to the independent film center in Hartford. When I saw the billing, it felt like a tornado had seized my brain and continued its path down my body, collecting and dizzying each organ, then spitting them out again. I found the side of a brick building to steady myself. If it had just been Celia's and Rafael's names, I might have second-guessed the odds. It was the film's title, *Os Bandidos da Noite*, that cemented the truth. They had stolen everything from Karina, even her name, capitalized on it, and made their betrayal known to the world.

I did go to the next screening. I bought a small bag of popcorn and a cream soda. I sat in the back corner and surveyed the audience, counted their ages, the number of couples, how many women had attended, watched their reactions, and then waited until they all left the theater before I cried.

The film was about a renegade, played by Rafael, who lives in the mountains outside of Lima. He captures a local Peruvian woman from her home and forces her to live as his accomplice, robbing homes for food and supplies, hiking south on the Andes to reach Bolivia, where he promised her he owned an alpaca farm where they would live. They seemingly become lovers, and even make love on the trail, until one day the woman kills him. A sharp rock to the neck. She had been secretly plotting his death the entire film, but her biggest obstacle was a moral one: she was a pacifist.

I hated the film, but I saw it several times. Celia was the director, and so I thought maybe I could study Rafael through her eyes. I wanted to see what she saw; I wanted to understand what made her love him. But I could only see the person at her apartment, eager to impress me with his Americanness, his tattooed symbols of regret, and poor Karina latched on to him, trying to keep him within her reach. Each time I left feeling more unsatisfied than when I walked in. After a few weeks they stopped showing *Os Bandidos da Noite,* and I never saw it again.

Simone didn't mention the movie when she told me about Rafael and Celia. The only other news she had was that Celia had left their theater company without warning and the owner, who was an alcoholic and relied on Celia to handle the logistics, almost closed its doors.

"It was a very sad time, but we were able to organize, all the actors, the writers."

She adjusted a strap on her dress that had fallen down her shoulder and, in doing so, noticed that Hugo, who was staggering across the room, had seen her talking. She told me she had to keep circling.

"That's my job." She laughed. "Circle, circle, circle." And she turned in to the crowd.

I had imagined many times how I might see Celia again. One vision I had was that she'd be waiting at the airport gate as we boarded the plane for the U.S. Sometimes while sitting in the apartment I'd have an uncanny feeling that she was about to walk through the door. I saw the backs of women whom I'd mistaken for Celia and I'd be hit with excitement, anxiety, and then disappointment. I once thought I saw Rafael and Celia in Ibirapuera park by a tree, a guitar leaned against his leg. But it was never her. I'd been floating inside my head, inventing scenarios for months. It was over. I filed through the crowd, past Baroque paintings and Grecian statues. I went to go find you.

You were standing near the rabbit statue, tipping the last of a champagne flute into your mouth. Before I had even approached you, I could tell you were angry—the way your shoulders curved back and your chest extended forward, like you were about to drum on it with two fists.

"Dennis," I said. "What's the matter?"

You tilted your eyes at me.

"We should go," you said.

"Where are Eduardo and Melinda? Have you seen them?"

You yelled a loud *"Ha!"* and several people glanced over at you. "I've seen Eduardo. The Provost." You said "the Provost" with four fingers wagging through the air in quotes.

"What happened?" I tried to put my hand on your shoulder, but you shook it away.

"That fucker."

"Which fucker? Eduardo?"

"I don't even want to hear his name!" You curved and flexed your hands and began to pace within a contained radius. "He made me work day and night to write that goddamn article. Weekends, nights, vacations. All time I could have saved. All time I could have had back. All time I could have spent with y—" Your voice broke before you could finish the sentence.

"He's not publishing the article," I said, almost to myself.

"You know what— Fuck Eduardo. Fuck this job. Fuck being somebody's lackey!"

As you said this, your arm swept around and, with the force of countless minutes spent suppressing, hoarding, fending off your rage, you struck the bunny rabbit off its pedestal and propelled it onto the floor.

It smashed. Its small red head rolled to the feet of a growing crowd of bystanders. They fell silent and then gasped. I even saw one man collapse onto his hands and knees.

I stood frozen, but you had thawed. You took my hand and we hurried as fast as possible toward the exit.

Hugo was leaving the bathroom, so when he saw the frantic

crowd around his rabbit, he charged through, his belly plowing the path. Someone must have pointed at you as the culprit, so he pivoted and ran, caught up to us, and grabbed your jacket. He began yelling obscenities at you, words that I have blocked from my memory but that caused several people to cover their ears.

"Do you realize what you've done?" he said. "You will pay for this for the rest of your life!"

You looked like you were going to scream back, your mouth slackened, your eyes zeroed in, the way you do when you're about to serve an intellectual walloping. But you didn't say anything. Instead, you hardened your fist, wound your shoulder, and punched him across his jaw.

The Provost and Melinda didn't see you hit him, but they did see us leave. In many ways that rabbit saved us. After steadying from the blow, Hugo was too distraught by the broken bunny to try to find you again. I saw Simone near the coatroom on our way out and tried to grab her attention, but she noticeably avoided me, staying clear from the commotion.

On the bus home your knuckles looked pale, drained of blood.

"It's nothing," you said, cradling one hand in the other. I could see the tears mounting.

"I know Hugo instigated it," I said. "And I don't blame you. But did you really have to hit him?"

You turned and stared out at the passing streetlights.

"I'm more worried about the rabbit. How are we going to pay for that?"

I paused.

"Should I start looking at flights?"

When we arrived home, we already had four missed calls from the Provost and a voicemail asking you to call him.

"Do you feel like talking?" I said. "Maybe you should wait until the morning."

You didn't answer me; you went to the kitchen and dialed. I left for the bedroom and tried not to listen to the hum of your voice from the other side of the door.

The receiver clicked; the refrigerator opened and shut. You walked into the bedroom with your shirt undone, drinking a glass of mango juice. The edges formed a pink smile around your mouth.

I made a cold compress in the bathroom and placed it on your knuckles.

"How did it go?" I asked.

"He called to see if I was all right. Someone told him that Hugo had lunged at me." You took another gulp. "Linda, the rabbit wasn't even real. It was a replica. It's barely worth anything. I explained that it was an accident, a misunderstanding . . ." You trailed off. "Eduardo said he would cover the costs, he's so embarrassed by how Hugo reacted."

You lay down on top of the sheets and closed your eyes. I could see the night's events replaying in your thoughts. I curled up next to you, hugging your shoulder. Maybe it was the equal but opposite force—my action against your action—that began to level the tension. Or maybe we had exhausted each other so much that we had no choice but to let go.

"I'm sorry," I said, my mouth close to your ear. I could see the deep blue impressions under your eyelids, the pink flush that had sucked up the life in your cheeks, the numbness, like a slab of black licorice, that had become your stare.

You shook your head then looked at me, pressed your forehead against mine.

"I'm sorry I left you," I said again.

You whispered, Let's stay like this for a while, and I whispered back, I'll stay here for as long as you want. You had a just-woken tenderness tucked in the crook of your neck, and I wondered how I could expand this tender place, the small cradle where you stored your limitlessness, your empathy, your capacity to learn and not just teach. Had you given up or given in? I was too afraid to ask. I wanted to rest into this place, find a way to stretch my arms and legs there, to make the uncomfortable a little more comfortable. Maybe we could do it together.

We stayed like this until the morning, two birds folded into each other, savoring the growing warmth between us, no noise except for the blow of your exhale against my shoulder. We were beginning to dissolve; we had turned stone into liquid; we were shaping our broken branch into a boat that, eventually, would float us down the river, toward forgiveness.

Chapter Twenty-seven

We spent a summer in winter, but spring is always a rebirth, even when it's autumn in Brazil. Celia had been in Peru for four months already, probably living out of Rafael's car, searching for camera shops that developed 35-millimeter film. We had lived through the turn of the New Year, which we spent with a carton of raspberry sorbet at our apartment, watching fireworks burst above the park. We survived Carnaval and the green feathers and glitter floating through our living room window. We managed the start of a new semester, you returning to teach, and I reassimilated to an apartment with just me and Marta.

I picked up painting again, here and there, but mostly I spent my time writing again. I was becoming reacquainted with putting my thoughts down on the page. I wrote early in the morning and before we went to bed in a sage green notebook that my father gave me on my thirtieth birthday. I tore out the pages where I had scribbled down lists and scheduling plans, and began to record the things I didn't want to forget, the memories that would eventually evolve into this story to you.

During the day, Melinda invited me to come to her athletic club to go swimming, which was the most ideal way to spend time with Melinda—swimming next to her in an adjacent lane. Sometimes we went as often as five days a week. After our swim we'd eat lunch at the club café, which sold expensive sandwiches and sliced fruit in plastic boxes. I enjoyed our routine—we didn't have to speak while we swam, and she couldn't smoke or drink wine there, which meant our lunches were the right balance of short and sober.

When I first started swimming, my mind would flip to thoughts about Celia. I'd replay conversations, think about how I could have said something differently, said something more, said less, touched her more, repented. The thoughts would continue until I veered into another lane and collided with a swimmer, or hit the crown of my head against the pool wall. One time I hit my head so hard I thought I might faint. I held on to the cement staircase and let the black wash over my eyes. I passed my tongue across my lips to taste if any blood had mixed into the chlorine. When I realized I was fine—that my vision would return, that my head wasn't bleeding—I pivoted and continued to swim.

The more I swam, the stronger I became. Each week I accumulated laps without stopping, and found it easier to turn and start a new set instead of clutching on to the ledge to catch my breath. I learned how to pay more attention. I counted strokes so that I knew when it was time to dive and twist and push my feet against the tiles. My breath became rhythmic—stroke, stroke, breathe, stroke, stroke, breathe—so that when I broke the surface, a buzz of oxygen lifted me across the water.

You and I still hadn't become physically intimate, but after a couple more months we would find each other again, you would smooth the curves of my stronger body, I would kiss the freshness of your newly shaven cheeks. But for now, we were learning how to speak to each other. We spent the evenings lying in bed face-to-face, hands clutched, reflecting on the contradictory world we would return to in the United States. There would be no weapons of mass destruction. The Red Sox would finally win the World Series. New Orleans would be underwater.

During this uncertain time, Marta was an unwavering presence. She still arrived every day at 9:00 A.M., cleaned, cooked, ate lunch in the laundry room closet, listened to soap operas, and left at 3:00 P.M. wearing her church clothes. It was as though there was never a time before Marta, and there would never be a time after. She was the essential, the intangible, the very core of us.

Then one day I did see a change in her. She was vacuuming in the living room when suddenly she stopped and sat down on the couch. I glanced at her from the kitchen—she held her chin in her hands and stared out the window. This listlessness passed through her for days. I would catch her standing at the mirror or the kitchen sink, blank with thought, her eyes lost inside her mind, until she noticed me notice her and would snap back into place.

I looked for signs of malaise. I couldn't find anything physical, but her uncharacteristic distraction continued. She left the iron flat on my blouse and burned a small brown triangle on the collar. Burning became a pattern—she left a casserole in the oven for three hours; she boiled coffee on the stove until it was as thick as molasses; she singed her forehead with the curling iron, leaving a red stripe above her brow.

Later that week I found her on the telephone in the laundry room, pressed up against the washing machine. As soon as I walked in she rushed to hang up, apologized to me repeatedly— desculpa, desculpa—and fled into the living room with her hands flying, explaining that she had to call her sister, that she didn't have her calling card, that she never usually used the house phone but it was very important and that she would pay us back.

"I don't care about the phone," I told her. "What's going on?"

"Nothing," she said. "Family things."

She didn't say more and I didn't pry. She cooked dinner and packed it into the refrigerator, then changed in her room. But before she left for the day, she approached me again, her arms tight by her sides.

"Okay. There is something."

"What is it?"

"I have a tumor in my breast."

At first I thought, hoped, that maybe she'd used the wrong word. Did she mean tenderness? Tension? No, she said. She meant tumor.

"How big is it?" I asked. I went to reach for her, but she didn't respond. "How long have you known?"

"It's very small. The size of a small stone. They will cut my breast and then I will be done." As she said this she formed scissors with her fingers and motioned to the area where they would cut. "Not the whole breast. A piece."

I tried to imagine the beige-pink matter growing inside her, a spiderweb of cells that had inhabited her while she cooked food and washed bowls and folded laundry.

"When is the surgery?" I asked.

"Next week."

"That's so soon," I said, and we both paused, looked down at the floor.

"What day?"

"Wednesday," she said. "Quarta-feira."

"How long will you be gone?"

"I want to be back in three weeks," she said and, perhaps sensing my panic, she clarified, "I will be back in three weeks."

She gave me a short hug when she saw my tears, then took her bag and left. Her sister was waiting downstairs.

I noticed Marta's absence in the presence of myself. I would put a dish in the sink in the morning and it would still be there at night. I went through a week of underwear until I remembered I had to do the laundry. So much of Marta's power was untraceable to the naked eye. She had carefully maintained order in the apartment, erased our messy paths, so that I barely noticed we had one.

You received the news harder than I thought you would.

"What does she need? Should we give her money?"

"She wouldn't accept it," I said. "She's being treated for free under the Brazilian healthcare system."

"I'm going to miss her."

I wrapped my arms around your back. "She'll be back. Marta will outlive us all."

That night I studied my own breasts in the bathroom mirror. They had firmed from swimming but were still soft enough to droop. I pressed them up and let them fall. You touched my breasts so gently it sometimes tickled. Celia pressed them against her open mouth, hard, and I worried that she'd leave a mark. I put my shirt back on and folded my arms across my chest. I hoped that I would never need strangers to hold them, cut into them, throw them away in a metal can.

"I don't want her to die," I said to you the following morning. I had woken up thinking only about the possibility of Marta's death.

"She's not going to die."

"How do you know?"

"She told you herself—the tumor is very small. They caught it early. She'll have surgery and maybe radiation, and then she'll be done."

"I wish I could speak to the doctor," I said, and leaned against the washing machine just outside her room, staring, until the coffee in my mug went cold.

Chapter Twenty-eight

We had decided that three weeks wasn't enough time to recover. Still, three weeks after her surgery, Marta called the apartment. She wanted to return. She told me that she had this feeling she had forgotten something, but what it was she couldn't remember. It was clawing at her thoughts, she told me, this forgetful feeling, and she kept waking up in the night wondering, What did I forget? Did I leave my purse? My keys? My Bible?

"It's too soon for you to work," I told her. "Your body needs time to heal."

"I won't work. I want to search the apartment, and then I'll leave."

I said she could come look, and she arrived the next day early in the morning. Her arrival coincided with Melinda and Eduardo's departure for a series of conferences in Europe. The trip could last for as long as a month, they said, and I couldn't go to the pool without Melinda. You and I went out together to buy flowers and a cake for Marta's arrival and set them up decoratively on the kitchen table.

When Marta walked through the door, the first thing I noticed was how different she looked. Yes, the bandages had flattened her breasts so that she lacked voluminousness, but she also looked worn. Her face had formed new creases and wrinkles, as though something were sucking acutely from the inside. She turned without moving her shoulders—the slightest twist or bend could push open her incision.

I asked her if she wanted to sit for a moment, but she was anxious to begin looking for what she'd lost. She went first to the laundry room and I heard her shifting her belongings on the shelves, then she came back to the kitchen, opened cabinets, removed cutlery and coffee cups, replaced them when nothing surfaced.

"Maybe you forgot it on the bus?" I asked.

She bent down cautiously to rummage under the sink.

"I'm sure it's here."

Eventually I left her alone. I realized that, in this moment, it was more important that she be autonomous in the apartment than it was for me to stay by her side. I buried myself in a magazine, ignoring the clanging sounds of pots and pans, until a sharp smell hit my nose—it had traveled all the way to the bedroom—and I realized she had turned on the gas stove.

I watched her from the kitchen door as she boiled a pot of water.

"Marta? What are you doing?"

"I couldn't find it," she said. "I brought fresh vegetables from the feira in Atibaia that I thought I would cook."

"But, the doctor says you're not supposed to work yet."

"I'm not working," she said and poured a cup of rice into the water.

I hadn't realized how much I'd grown to miss Marta's lunches, the waxy fragrance of onions and rice, tomatoes and salt, black beans and bay leaves, until the smell surrounded me again. I even missed her margarine spread inside a dinner roll, as vibrant as a daffodil, that tasted both salty and sweet.

She arranged a platter with sliced tomatoes, chopped red onions, and yucca powder, which I mixed into my bowl of rice and beans. I ate without stopping. The only thought that passed my mind was how delicious the tomato was, so firm and flavorful, it barely even needed salt. When I finished she collected my plate and went to her room for a rest, she told me, before she headed home.

As soon as she got on the bed she let out a deep moan. It was more like a voiced exhale, an exorcised rumble, long and low but loud enough to hear through a closed door.

I peeked inside the laundry room.

"Was that you?" She was halfway sitting on her mattress, adjusting knobs on the radio.

"Yes," she said. "I yawned."

I told her that she should go home, that I would clean up after lunch and pack her a plate to take home.

"I don't want to see you here for another two weeks. You need more time to recover."

She agreed and, after a short nap, left for the bus station.

She returned the following week. You had just left for work and I assumed you'd returned for a textbook you forgot. I wasn't expecting Marta.

"You're back?" I said.

She was visibly shaken. I asked her how she was feeling.

"I feel fine," she said. "I can't sit at home anymore or else I'll go crazy. I'm coming back to work."

I didn't want to debate with her. She handed me a bag of figs she had brought with her. I sat at the kitchen table and popped and peeled the fig skins while she swept the kitchen floor.

That was the second time I heard the moan. Marta tilted her head down and steadied her hands on her hips. I kept asking her if she needed to stop working and take a rest, but every time she insisted she was fine.

"Dennis, I don't know what to do," I said when you returned home from work.

"What's wrong?" You opened the refrigerator door and stood in the cool air.

"It's Marta. She's in so much pain, but she keeps working. I'm worried she's going to hurt herself."

"I know it's hard, but that's her decision to make."

"If her only choices are between work and sitting at home, that's not much of a decision." I left to take a cold rinse in the shower.

As I placed my hand under the running shower water, trying to feel for the right temperature, I thought about the first time I had to give my father a bath. By that point he had no memory of who I was—before I arrived at his house, depending on his mood, the hospice nurse would either explain that his daughter or a kind young woman was coming to keep him company. Of course, I remembered everything about my father. I remembered how, as a child, I could grab on to his forearm with both my hands and swing. I remembered how he drank beer with pasta. I remembered him suspended on a power line, high up in the air.

Now his bones and skin were light and loose, like the underside of a dog's snout. I was embarrassed thinking that I would have to see him naked, embarrassed for him and for me, and I kept trying to come up with maneuvers in my head so that I wouldn't face him front-on. When I arrived, he was on the sofa watching *M*A*S*H*. The hospice nurse, Philomene, had to leave to take her daughter to a school dance. I gave her a hug goodbye and sat next to my father on the sofa. We were silent for a while, staring at the television, and then I told him that I was going to draw the water. I was nervous. He looked frightened too. I turned to him and stroked his hair, fine like corn silk, and told him that it would be all right. Everything was new to him again, but not new with a childlike wonder: new with a very adult sense of anxiety and paranoia. I rubbed the tops of his bumpy hands, traced with blue veins, until he initiated standing and we walked to the bathroom together. I helped him step out of his pants, pull his shirt over his head, and folded them neatly on top of the toilet seat, as he had done since he was a boy. Then he stepped into the tub himself, looked up at me with his smoky green eyes, and told me that the water felt fine.

Though his memory had all but vanished, his body still remembered how beautiful it feels to be cared for. He laughed and smiled when I took the sponge and squeezed it onto his back and over the top of his head. He stood up and I wrapped him in a towel, as he had done for me when I was a little girl, and he let me brush his hair. I gave him a pack of Junior Mints and he ate them as I massaged his shoulders, which had bowed into slender arches over the years. It's a moment I'll remember for the rest of my life, whether I actually remember it or not.

The next morning, before Marta arrived, I set up a line of tea candles along our bathtub ledge. I laid out my bathrobe on the sink and dripped eucalyptus oil into the white porcelain tub. I drew a hot bath, so hot the room filled with a fragrant steam. I set up a radio in the corner and turned on the classical station, which was playing a Bach violin concerto, then laid out a tray with cookies and cold green tea. When Marta arrived, the water had reached a golden, refreshing temperature. I led her into the bathroom.

"Soak for hours," I said. "For as long as you want. If the water goes cold, drain it and start again." I told her to call me if she needed anything else.

At first she hesitated, in the way of polite refusal. But when I shut the door I heard her laugh. And then, an hour later, when she was still inside, I heard her laugh again. It made me laugh too.

Chapter Twenty-nine

I heard you shout from the kitchen, "The taxi isn't coming." You were on the phone with the Provost, who had called between meetings to make sure we were on schedule for our flight home. We had shipped our belongings the week prior. All we had left were two suitcases and our toothbrushes resting on the bathroom sink.

"I called three hours ago to reserve it and it's still not here," you said into the receiver, and then, Okay, okay, and hung up.

Marta was with us cleaning for the next residents, an oncologist from Switzerland and her wife, who were due to arrive in a few days.

"I don't know what to do," you said to me, exasperated, holding one hand to your forehead. "The Provost is going to try and find us his driver, but at this rate, even if he came immediately, we'd still miss our flight."

We had had little opportunity to digest our departure; the last few days had been cluttered with logistics. We kept misplacing everything we needed: our passports, the keys to our house in Hartford, your leaving papers from the university, my immigration documents. Marta kept us organized as best she could, stacking the essentials by the door as soon as they were found. Her incision had healed and she was waiting to hear from the doctors whether she needed radiation. She had a checkup the following week, and I made her promise that she would call to tell us what she learned. Her niece had already begun to stock wigs at her salon, just in case. From what I could see she moved ably, perhaps more ably now than she had before. Her walk had a particular lightness, a starry buoyancy, as though the physical loss had made her spiritually new.

You and Marta had developed a special bond in the final weeks we were together. I listened to your conversations from the other side of the wall, how she spoke about her relationships at home, with the church and with her family. You told her you were nervous about forgetting the small pleasures that you had grown to love in Brazil, pleasures that would surely evaporate with time. The rich tang of the coffee, the wisp of a storm wind on a humid afternoon, the students who shared with you their personal histories, how beer in São Paulo was served so cold the cans would burn your lips.

Your nostalgia, already clearly formed, made me wonder why we were leaving at all. Why not stay? The Provost would, without a doubt, hire you full-time. I could contact Simone—maybe I could take Celia's old job at the theater. We would find a way. Why did we have to leave? The issue with the taxi seemed like the last opportunity to abandon this destiny, and for a moment I thought maybe it was a sign that we weren't meant to go, that the country wanted us to stay.

And then the time arrived. I took a breath and remembered that even permanence isn't lasting. São Paulo would always be here, still evolving, when we decided to return.

Marta came into the living room, dragging our two suitcases behind her.

"Come," she said. "My sister is downstairs. She will take you to the airport."

I hadn't expected to ever meet Felina, the bridge that connected Marta between her two worlds, our lives and theirs. When I saw her sitting outside our apartment in a gray Toyota Camry, a wooden rosary hanging from the rearview mirror, I felt Marta's entire life had materialized in an instant.

"Oi!" she said and cranked the emergency brake, hopped out of the car, and gave us both a hug and a kiss. She made room for us in the backseat, put a dog kennel in the trunk, and swept a few empty bottles of Guaraná to the floor, so that we all managed to fit.

This was Felina. She sounded like a song when she spoke with Marta, repeatedly tucking her hair behind her ears as she drove, her attention shared between her sister and the road. The sky opened to a warm sun that splayed across my knees and arms. Felina rolled down her window and opened her palm against the blowing wind, occasionally diving her hand like a river dolphin. Through the gusts I could make out the radio, faintly, playing Elis Regina. Marta hummed along.

When we arrived at the airport, Felina left us with a final hello and goodbye, this time three kisses for each. The passenger side door cracked and Marta stepped out.

"Tchau," she said and hugged me, pressing the side of her mouth against my cheek. When I thought she might let go, she held on for a few seconds longer. I felt the sorrow burning my nose and my eyelids. I almost let the tears fall, but then I saw Felina and Marta exchange an ancestral smirk, one that can only pass between sisters, and my sadness lifted. They waved to us from the window, Felina blowing kisses as they drove off together, a puff of smoke hovering in the car's wake. You took my bag, and I followed you through sliding glass doors. We were on our way home.

Acknowledgments

Mom: Thank you for valuing art and thus teaching me to. Thank you for giving me a connection to Brazil. For offering to hand out flyers and sell copies of my book out of the trunk of your car. I love you.

Karina, Simone, Aunt Lili: When I met you again, as an adult, it was like a hidden part of me opened up. Thank you for showing me São Paulo and Atibaia, for sharing your life with me. Thank you for the late nights, the philosophizing, the singing and dancing, all of which is the soul of this book. Saudades. Eu amo vocês.

Nicole Counts: Thank you for your heart and for your mind. Thank you for challenging me and for seeing me. For contemplating life with me over breakfast. This book is yours, too.

Marya Spence: Thank you for being the best agent in the business. For your patience, your love of literature, your empathy, and your shine. I am lucky you always listen to my long, rambling voice messages.

The One World/Random House team: I feel so much gratitude for all of you. Thank you for treating me and my book with such dignity and care.

Flora Medawar, my sister: Thank you for the many years of joy and friendship. We'll still be laughing when we're wrinkled, wreaking havoc in matching golf carts.

Avis Skinner: Thank you for being such an important pillar in my life.

Sumitra Rajkumar, my dear friend and writing comrade: Thank you for understanding the pleasure and pain in writing. Thank you for contemplating it with me over countless dinners, drinks, writing circles, texts, and voice messages. We share in this journey together. (And thanks for Rob Quatrone, too.)

Kelly Castagnaro and Karen Good Marable: Thank you for being my writing sisters-in-arms. Thank you for always coming through with the strength and wisdom.

John Glynn: Thank you for telling me that it was possible before I believed it was. For going first and letting me learn from you. For providing the industry insight. Thank you.

Blakney Young, Mira Jube, Claire Minihan, Amelia O'Connor: Thank you for the group chats and island times. For listening to me as I found my way. You are the best of friends.

You too, Hannah Hawkins.

Wei Tchou and Sam Cohen: I'm so grateful that 2020 at least brought me your friendships.

Lauren Malinowski: We are #olddogs for life.

Pavan Dhillon: Thank you for feeding me your mother's Indian food after work. For calling me from San Francisco. For your friendship during those MFA days. Thank you.

GLOW, aka Glorious Ladies of Writing: Thank you for the early-on friendship and community.

To the teachers who shaped me, especially Anne Phaneuf, Justin Torres, Jackson Taylor, and Flaminia Ocampo: Learning from you made all the difference to me. Thank you.

Anna Burnham, my sister: This book is dedicated to you because I couldn't have written it without you. Thank you for being my sister, friend, ally, neighbor, and family. I love you.

And to Emil Hafeez, the true love of my life: You are in every word I write. Thank you for you. I love you.

GABRIELLA BURNHAM is a dual citizen of the United States and Brazil. Now a New York resident, she lived in São Paulo as a child and most of her family still lives there today. She holds an MFA in creative writing from The Writer's Foundry at St. Joseph's College and has been awarded fellowships to MacDowell and Yaddo. She has worked as a reporter, a creative writing teacher, and in immigration law. *It Is Wood, It Is Stone* is her first novel.